"MISS TEENAGE AMERICA, HUH?"

April just stood there, mouth open. What had she done to deserve *that?"*

Before she could recover, she felt a hard, thudding blow that pushed her backward against her locker.

Half dazed, April stared at the boys. Some of them wore white T-shirts tucked into cuffed jeans. Others wore wide black leather belts hung with chains. But they all had razor-short hair and tattoos of dragons on their arms.

Skinheads, April realized with a shudder. She had seen people like them on the television news.

She didn't wait another minute. She hurried away down the hall.

"Aw, we scared the little girl," raspy voices called after her.

It was all she could do not to break into a run . . .

CROSSTOWN

KATHRYN MAKRIS

AN AVON FLARE BOOK

CROSSTOWN is an original publication of Avon Books. This work has never before appeared in book form.

AVON BOOKS
A division of
The Hearst Corporation
1350 Avenue of the Americas
New York, New York 10019

Copyright © 1993 by Kathryn Makris
Published by arrangement with the author
Library of Congress Catalog Card Number: 92-97438
ISBN: 0-380-76226-9
RL: 5.7

First Avon Flare Printing: June 1993

AVON TRADEMARK REG. U.S. PAT. OFF. AND IN OTHER COUNTRIES, MARCA REGISTRADA, HECHO EN CANADA

Printed in Canada

UNV 10 9 8 7 6 5 4 3 2

For my teachers
with special thanks to
Mrs. Eastus, Dr. Hendrix, and Dr. Mooney

Chapter 1

"Come on, April. You look fine."

"No, I don't. My hair. Look at it." April Morgan pulled a honey-blond curl off her shoulder and aimed a bottle of hair spray at it. The spray might fix her hair, but there didn't seem to be much she could do about the butterflies in her stomach.

Her friend, Toby Hubble, sighed. "Your hair is perfect. *You're* perfect. What more do you want? Long legs, cute nose, even turquoise eyes, for heaven's sake." Toby glanced in the mirror and took a poke at her own brown hair, cut in a pageboy around her plump face. "And I'll bet a million dollars you made Pep Squad. But if you're not there when they announce it, they might just un-elect you. Let's go!"

April dabbed on a last bit of lipstick, then followed her friend out.

Calm down, she told herself. Toby was right. It was silly to get so worked up about a Pep Squad election. April hoped she would win a spot, but if she didn't, so what? There were lots more important things in life. At the moment, though, it was hard to keep those things in mind.

"Oh, there you are!" Lauren Frede called to them in the hall. "Everybody's wondering where you've been, April. We're all in the gym already. Oh, gosh." She looked at the gold watch on her slender wrist. "The

1

announcements are only fifteen minutes away. I'm so nervous.''

"You two are making *me* nervous, and I didn't even run for Pep Squad." Toby rolled her eyes. "I'm sure you both made it, okay? Just don't have your heart attacks before the announcements, because then you won't live to hear about it.'' She gave her friends little shoves to propel them into the gym.

The bleachers were packed with an all-school assembly. Voices and laughter echoed off the new gym's gleaming floors and high, arched ceiling.

All these people, April thought. Some had voted for her. Others hadn't. But lots of kids had encouraged April to run. Even the friends of other candidates were really nice about it. No one got vicious or catty about Pep Squad elections. That's just not how things worked at Covington High. People were good sports. April tried to keep that in mind as head after head turned to watch her and Lauren walk in. Naturally, she told herself, people would be curious about the candidates. *How nervous are they? Will they cry if they lose? Cry if they win?* The important thing, though, was that it was all among friends. That's what counted.

April smiled at everyone along the aisle. Even so, the butterflies in her stomach were turning into jumbo jets.

The gym was a riot of color. Banners of Covington High's royal-blue and gold draped the walls, and blue and gold balloons bobbed everywhere. Sunshine streamed in through the skylights.

The sun's warmth made April feel better. When she saw a group of her friends sitting in the first couple of rows of bleachers, her spirits rose even higher.

Andrea Nelson, a senior Pep Squad member, got up to greet them. "Hi! Where've you been? Come sit down.''

Neither Andrea nor the other seniors on the squad had to worry about reelection. Only a half dozen junior and

2

sophomore spots were up for a vote that fall. But Andrea looked as anxious as the rest of them.

Toby led the way to seats in the second row. Just as they sat down, April felt a jab in the ribs.

Lauren pointed at Jenette Wright, the Pep Squad captain, smiling back at them from the first row. Lauren waved with one of her long, carrot-red braids, and April smiled.

"Jenette is so great!" Lauren whispered. "Oh, gosh, I hope we're elected."

April nodded. "Me, too. But if we're not, there *is* life after the Pep Squad elections, right?"

"That's the spirit," Toby agreed.

Wilsey Carr reached back from her seat in front of them to pat April and Lauren on the knees. "Everybody I know voted for you. My brother says the whole football team did, too."

Lauren glanced over her shoulder at Wilsey's brother, Jake, and his teammates sitting a few rows behind them. "Oh, my gosh, April. He's looking at you."

"Who is?"

Toby whispered, *"Him."*

"Garrett Martin!" Wilsey narrowed her dark eyes. "When are you going to get it through your head that he likes you, April?"

"No, he doesn't." April giggled.

"Yes, he does, you dope." Lauren leaned closer. "He told Jake he does."

"He did?" April asked Wilsey.

Wilsey nodded. "I was going to tell you after the announcements. Oh! Oh, wow!" She froze, staring at the rows behind April.

"What?" Toby turned to look. Then she turned back, giggling and nudging April. "He's coming."

"Garrett? He's coming over *here?*"

"Yes!" hissed Lauren. "Oh, my gosh!"

3

April's cheeks went red-hot. "You're kidding, aren't you?"

"Hey there." The voice came from right behind April. "Got your fingers crossed?"

She turned her head slightly. Garrett Martin gave her a huge, spectacular grin.

"April doesn't need to cross her fingers," said Toby. "She's got it in the bag."

"Bet you're right," agreed Garrett. *"I* voted for you."

April turned a bit more, and smiled. "You did?"

"How about me?" Lauren asked, popping her chewing gum. "You better have voted for *me,* too."

"Yeah, matter of fact, I did." Garrett nodded, then wedged a knee between April and Toby. "Mind if I sit here?"

"Be my guest," said Toby, grinning.

Garrett squeezed his large frame in beside April. Her heart hammered. She had never sat so close to him before. Lately he had been talking to her at lunch. But he was a senior, a football hero, and one of the most popular guys at Covington. April couldn't believe he was paying attention to her, just a sophomore.

"You're not nervous, are you?" he asked.

Light-headed, April could barely speak. Garrett was *so* gorgeous. He was grinning at her sideways, chestnut hair curling around his tanned face, eyes the blue of a bright summer sky.

Finally, she laughed. *"Very* nervous."

He patted her shoulder. "You shouldn't be." His hand lingered on her shoulder a moment, then slipped around her waist. "You're a winner."

A tingle raced through April. It would be easy to take Garrett at his word. His arm around her was almost enough to make her forget all about the Pep Squad elections and the hundreds of Covington High students around them.

4

She leaned against him a little. "Easy for you to say."

He gave her another grin.

"Shh! Rutherford's going to the mike," warned Wilsey.

The gym started to quiet down as the principal headed for the podium set up at half-court.

"Oh, gosh, she's wearing that polyester pantsuit again," whispered Lauren. "I hate that thing. Doesn't she own anything made after 1975?"

"It's better than the blue plaid dress. You know, the one with the matching cape?" Toby wrinkled her nose.

April took a deep breath, trying to stay calm about the fact that Garrett Martin still had his arm around her.

"Good afternoon, people. Thank you all for assembling quietly," Mrs. Rutherford began.

Toby yawned, then started droning along with the principal, "And thank you for respecting our rules prohibiting food and beverages in the gymnasium . . ."

April giggled. "Toby, hush."

Lauren chimed in. ". . . and for depositing your litter in the trash receptacles."

"That woman deserves a prize," whispered Wilsey. "Least original speaker."

April nodded. "The broken-record award."

"Rewind, replay," added Lauren.

Garrett gave April a squeeze. "You don't seem nervous anymore."

"That's what friends are for." Toby winked.

"And now we approach the moment you've all been waiting for," Mrs. Rutherford was saying. She adjusted her glasses. "As you know, this assembly was called for a very special set of announcements. Yesterday you voted for this year's sophomore and junior Pep Squad members. Today the squad captain, Jenette Wright, will give you the results of that election. The Pep Squad is an integral part of Covington Senior High. Its young women are model members of our community."

"I wish she'd get *on* with it," groaned Lauren.

"And with your vote you uphold Covington's high standards of citizenship and service. Well, without further ado, I'll turn over the podium to Jenette for the news I know you're all eager to hear." Mrs. Rutherford smiled broadly.

Jenette skipped across the gym floor to the podium. She wore the Pep Squad's coveted uniform—a slim-fitting royal-blue sweater and a short, flippy skirt in alternating panels of blue and gold. Her hair, long and lemon-blond, shone in the sunlight.

Several low whistles came from boys in the bleachers.

The next few minutes passed in a blur for April. She heard Jenette ask the audience to show their appreciation for all the Pep Squad candidates who worked so hard in the tryouts. She felt the light pressure of Garrett's arm around her waist, and saw the dancing blue and gold of the banners and balloons festooning the gym. Then Jenette started reading the names of the new junior Pep Squad members.

April's stomach jumped into action again, turning into a tightly knotted mess.

"Now, for the sophomores . . ." Jenette went on. "The first name is . . . Lauren—"

"Oh, my gosh!" screamed Lauren, even before Jenette could say her last name. She reached right across Garrett and grabbed April's hands.

"You're comin' up," Garrett assured April.

". . . Susan Lamar," Jenette announced next. "And our third sophomore is . . ."

Garrett traced little "V's" on April's back. V for victory. She closed her eyes. *Pep Squad is not the most important thing in the world. If I don't get it, it doesn't matter. It doesn't matter.*

In the next second, Lauren was screaming so loud that April could barely register what Jenette had said.

"Holy Toledo!" Toby yelled. "Way to go!" She jumped up and hugged April.

"You did it, babe," Garrett said, and kissed her.

In the soft light of the dining-room chandelier that evening, April held a little gold megaphone pendant. It dangled from a delicate gold chain that glistened against the background of her family's crystal goblets and white china.

"Isn't it beautiful?" she murmured.

"Let me see," her mother said.

April handed Mom the necklace. The afternoon's events had left her in a daze. It was all so wonderful—almost too wonderful to be true. But it *was* true, and she had set the family dinner table with their best to celebrate.

"It *is* beautiful, sweetheart," Mom smiled. "Really lovely." Her blue eyes stayed on the pendant in her palm, which rested open and limp on the table. Her whole body had looked that way all evening, kind of limp and disconnected.

Just tired, April decided. Mom had started a new job that month, as a secretary in a big law firm downtown. Since her divorce from Dad five years before, Mom had worked as the receptionist for a great old dentist right in Covington. But Dr. Dumas had just retired, so now Mom had a long commute to the city plus the stress of being new on the job.

"You're a cheerleader, huh?" asked April's little brother, Sean, between swallows of meat loaf. His wide, blue-green eyes, very much like her own, looked up at her through thick brown lashes.

"No, there are no cheerleaders at Covington High. We're Pep Squad members."

"Same thing, isn't it? You jump around and cheer and stuff." His sand-brown hair was messy, as usual. At least Mom had made him wash his face before dinner.

7

April pursed her lips. "Yes, we jump around and cheer at sports events. But we do a lot more than that. We represent our school in parades and other city functions, and we're supposed to be leaders at school and—"

"I wish you'd be in a sport instead," Sean interrupted. "Ross Macklin's sister is a cheerleader at Brookhurst, and she acts really stupid. Her friends come over and they practice these dumb dances."

"Routines," said April, trying to be patient. Nine-year-olds took a lot of patience. "They're called routines, and they're not dumb."

"*Very* dumb," her brother said.

"All right," said Mom. "That's enough, Sean. When you're in high school maybe you'll appreciate the Pep Team."

"Pep *Squad*," April corrected her.

"Sorry. Squad," Mom answered in a low voice, still looking at the necklace. She made a fist around it. "April . . ."

April looked up and saw tears in her mother's eyes.

"Mom?" she whispered. "What—?"

Her mother shook her head. She reached for her water goblet and took a long drink, then a long breath. Without looking, she handed the necklace to April. "I . . . um . . . There's some news."

"What?" April frowned.

"Well, you . . ." Her mother paused. "I'm terribly sorry, sweetheart. I shouldn't have waited so long. I should have told you earlier."

"Told me what?"

"I've been trying to find a solution, but . . . I wasn't able to, and . . . I'm so sorry. You can't be on the Pep Squad this year."

The gold chain felt cold in April's hand. She was sure she hadn't heard right.

"How come she can't?" asked Sean.

Mom looked at him, and then, finally, at April. "You

8

won't be able to keep attending Covington High this year, either, sweetheart.''

"What? What are you talking about, Mom?'' April's heart started to pound. This wasn't just a misunderstanding or a joke.

Her mother's blue eyes had gone lead-gray, and her chin trembled. "We have to move.''

"Move?'' echoed Sean. "Leave our house? Why do we have to move?''

"Because it . . . this isn't our house anymore, honey. I'm sorry. There have been some problems.''

"Mother, what problems?'' April demanded. "Will you please just tell us? This is scaring me.''

"I'm sorry, sweetheart. Don't be scared.'' Mom sighed, pushing a tuft of her frosted blond hair behind an ear. "Everything's under control, but we have to move, all right? The bank . . . the bank foreclosed on us, and—''

"What's foreclosed?'' asked Sean.

April gripped the necklace tight. This must be a nightmare. In a minute she would wake up and it would be over. The Pep Squad pendant, hard and solid and biting into her skin—that was the real part, wasn't it?

"Foreclosed,'' her mother said, "means that the house belongs to the bank now, because I couldn't keep up the payments on the loan.''

"You couldn't make our house payments?'' April barely recognized her own voice. She sounded like a croaking frog.

Mom pushed her hair behind her ears again, this time with both hands. She sat up straight and gazed back at her children. "No. I couldn't. I fell behind.''

"But why?'' asked April. "I mean, you're making just as much money as you did before.''

"Before,'' her mother said slowly, "I had a little extra to fall back on. But this year I'm over limit on the credit cards, and I bought the new car.''

9

"I thought you had plenty saved up for the car payments," said April, "and that's why we could afford to get a good one."

"I thought so, too." Mom folded her hands on the table.

No one was eating anymore.

April looked at Sean, whose bewilderment showed in his widened eyes.

"What about Dad?" April asked. "Can't he help?"

"Yeah!" Sean leaned forward. "He can send money!"

Mom shook her head. She stared into the china cabinet. "Your dad can't help right now. He hasn't been able to make the support payments for several months, because he has other expenses."

April tried to think through the dark fog that surrounded her head. She knew Dad had been late with his child-support checks. He lived in another part of the state with his new wife, Lacey, and her four-year-old son. They had just built a house on the edge of a forest, and Lacey was pregnant. Maybe that's what Mom meant when she said Dad had "other expenses."

Still, during the divorce he had promised in court to help Mom support April and Sean. Why wasn't he doing that now?

There had to be a solution. They couldn't leave their house, where they had lived since April was in kindergarten. And how could she leave Covington High? That was crazy! Mom had to be wrong about that part. Surely April could finish the year there, at least.

"Are we getting a new house?" Sean asked.

Smiling, Mom reached over to stroke the hair away from his eyes. "I've found an apartment for us. We're all set."

"An apartment? There aren't any apartments in Covington," April shook her head in confusion.

10

"I know, sweetheart. That's why we can't stay in Covington."

"But we've *got* to stay here. I mean, at least for the semester. We could just stay here, then we could look around and find something . . ."

"I've looked, sweetheart. And we do have to move. I'm sorry. I'm very, very sorry." Mom's face, prettily made-up as always, went pale. But her jaw had a strong, determined set to it.

April felt the haze around her thoughts burning away. Slowly, things grew clear and coldly, sharply real.

It was as if she had been dreaming. The whole day—winning the Pep Squad spot, kissing Garrett, saying yes afterward when he asked her to the Autumn Ball, even the quiet, happy family dinner—all that was just a dream.

Here was the real part, like a doubled-over, sick punch in the stomach.

"We have ten days," Mom said, "then we have to go."

Chapter 2

"Where's your new house?" Lauren asked. She sat in the sunny window seat of April's bedroom, wrapping the miniatures that stood on the shelf.

"Apartment," April corrected. "Mom says it's close to where she works. I haven't seen it yet."

Toby loaded another stack of April's books into a cardboard box on the bed. "Downtown? There are some pretty neighborhoods around there."

April nodded. "The apartment building she found accepts dogs. That's the good news." She scratched the fur behind Ranger's tall black ears. The German shepherd lay beside her at her desk, where she was emptying the drawers of her school papers.

"That's the *only* good news." Lauren's brown eyes looked misty. "I still can't believe you have to move."

"Me neither," added Toby, shaking her head.

April's eyes stung. She felt a sniffle coming, but kept packing. In a moment the tears dried. During the days since Mom had told her and Sean the news, April had done almost nothing but cry. Maybe, at last, she was all cried out.

"Is your mother *sure* she can't make a payment or something to keep your house?" Lauren asked.

April shook her head. "It's too late." She had already been over all this with her mother. Over and over. Mom had missed the payments for several months. Then the bank set deadline after deadline by when she had to make them up, and Mom didn't take any of the time limits seriously. It had been over a year. She thought the bank's loan officers would give her yet another chance. They didn't.

"How could she get so far behind? Couldn't she have talked to somebody?" Toby shrugged. "I mean, you always see those ads on TV about low-cost legal advice and everything."

"I don't know." April didn't want to talk about it anymore. She was sick of talking about it. She had listened to everything her mother had to say about the situation, and had asked her a million questions. They always ended up right back where they started: they had lost the house, they had to move, and they had to leave Covington.

Toby changed the subject. "Hey, what's this?" She held up a flattened, dried blue flower. "It fell out of a book."

12

Lauren giggled. "Oh, my gosh, don't you remember? Jimmy Wagner!"

"Wow! You mean, this is one of those flowers Jimmy used to give April at recess?" Toby turned her big, dimpled grin on April, then folded both hands over her heart. "Your first love!"

April rolled her eyes. "Jimmy Wagner was *not* my first love."

"Yes, he was," countered Lauren. "He followed you around like a puppy all through seventh grade!"

April laughed with her friends, thinking about how long the three of them had been pals. She had known Lauren since fifth grade, and Toby had moved in across the street three years ago. If she could count on anyone, it was Toby and Lauren. Having them around to help her pack made it bearable.

"I need to ask you guys a favor," April said.

"Yup." Toby fit the last book into the box and dusted off her hands. "What?"

"Well . . ." April took a breath. "Would you—would you please not tell anyone about *why* I have to move? Not even Wilsey."

Lauren shrugged. "Well, sure. But why not?"

April bit her bottom lip. "Would *you* want people to know you were getting kicked out of your house?" She tried to keep the bitter note out of her voice, but couldn't.

Toby nodded. "We understand, April. We won't tell anybody." She flopped down on the bed. "This is such a bummer. I wish your mother would let you move in with me for the semester. Even the year."

"I've already tried that one on her." April sighed.

"One question, okay?" Lauren propped her chin on a palm. "How come we can't tell Wilsey why you're moving, April? She's your friend, too."

"I know she is. But she and her brother tell each other everything, and then he goes and tells the whole football team . . ."

13

"Oh, I get it. You don't want Garrett to know." Lauren's freckles seemed to droop in sympathy.

"That's part of it," April admitted.

Toby said in a low voice, "April already told him she can't go with him to the ball."

"*What?*" Lauren's brown eyebrows flew upward. "Why, April? You can go! It doesn't matter if you go to Covington High or not . . ."

April shook her head. "I'll be too busy moving next Saturday. We'll be setting up the new apartment."

"So what?" Lauren persisted. "You can take time out on Saturday night. Oh, come on, April!"

April just shook her head again. This was another subject she didn't want to talk about. She didn't even want to think about it anymore.

The day before, when she had told Garrett she couldn't go with him to the dance, his whole face had changed. His blue eyes narrowed, and his mouth seemed to harden. He looked as if he thought April was planning to go with someone else instead. But as soon as she explained to him that she couldn't go to the dance at all—that she had to move—he relaxed and acted really concerned. He told her how sorry he was, and said they'd just have to go out another time.

"Where do you want these?" Toby was pointing at the row of prize ribbons from Ranger's dog-obedience matches pinned on the wall.

"In one of the empty shoe boxes over there, please. Thanks." April took a deep breath to pull herself together.

That was the best way. To just concentrate on packing, and not think about the real reason why she couldn't go to the ball.

A couple of hours later, Toby and Lauren had just left for home when April heard a crash in the dining room. She slammed the front door shut and ran down the hall

14

to find her mother on her knees next to the china cabinet.

"Mom, what happened?"

"A dinner plate," her mother answered. "It slipped out of my hands."

Fragments of white lay on the rug. Mom began to pick them up, one by one. A green bow held her hair at the nape of her neck, but thin wisps of it strayed out around her face. Her beige silk blouse and green skirt were rumpled. April noticed a run at the ankle of her stocking. She wondered why Mom hadn't bothered to change since her appointment at the bank after work.

Sean ran in with Ranger. "What was that?"

"Just a broken plate, honey," said Mom.

He knelt beside her and picked up one of the pieces. "Uh-oh. Your wedding china. I broke one of the cups when I was little. At Christmas, remember?"

Mom smiled. "I remember. Now we're even."

"It's okay, though, right?" Sean held the piece of delicate china up to the light and turned it around and around like a kaleidoscope. "You can buy a new one, just like we bought a new cup for the one I broke."

Mom nodded, but didn't answer.

April knew why. Although two years ago her mother had replaced a piece of china, this time she couldn't. The plates cost a lot of money. And right now they didn't have money. Not enough money to keep the house, barely enough to keep the new car, and certainly not enough to buy April a dress for the Autumn Ball.

April hadn't asked her mother about the dance. She knew what Mom's answer would be. Girls needed formals for it. April would also have needed new shoes, new dressy nylons, and a big boutonniere for Garrett. She had a savings account, but her mother had borrowed most of the money out of it three months ago.

That should have been a clue. Mom kept promising to pay it back, but never had. Other clues, too, now

15

seemed so obvious. Their summer's vacation in a lake cottage instead of the planned trip to Florida. Mom no longer getting her facials or her nails done, even trimming her hair herself. And when the clothes dryer broke last spring, Mom insisted that hanging laundry out to dry was much better for the environment, anyway.

April headed for the kitchen to get a broom. As she passed the dining-room table a piece of paper caught her eye. It had an address printed in large type at the top.

"125 Wilcox Avenue," April read aloud. "Is this our new apartment, Mom?" She read on. "Easton Arms Apartments."

"It's very spacious," Mom said.

April frowned. "It's not *in* Easton, is it?"

"Three bedrooms," her mother said. "Gas and water paid."

"Mom, we're not going to live in Easton, are we?"

"The Easton neighborhood has one of the best high schools in the city," Mom went on. "And the grade school is quite good, too."

"Easton is one of the worst neighborhoods in the city!" April burst out. "You said it yourself. Jenette invited us to watch her in a track meet there, and you wouldn't let me go."

"It's very well-patrolled now," replied her mother. "City officials have focused on cleaning it up. You see police cars everywhere."

"Right, because they *need* to be there!" cried April. "I can't believe this! I just can't believe—"

"You can't believe anything, can you?" her mother interrupted. Suddenly she focused on April, eyes sharp with anger. But her voice stayed cold and hollow. "Well, believe it, April. Wake up and accept it. We are moving. We are moving to the Easton Arms Apartments. Your whining isn't going to help us at all."

April was stunned. She felt as if her mother had slapped her. *Whining?* Her world was falling apart, and

16

she was supposed to just accept it? She hardly ever talked back to Mom. They'd had their arguments—mostly about unimportant things. But this was not unimportant.

The pain and frustration of the last few days boiled inside April to the point of steaming anger. She didn't know how much longer she could hold it in.

"Mother," April said, trying to act calm. "Please listen to me. We have to think about this. Easton is a terrible neighborhood. The schools there can't possibly be good ones. Have you really thought this through?"

Her mother stood up. She threw the shards of china into a trash can. "Yes, sweetheart, I've thought it through. Very carefully. It was the only affordable apartment I could find. This is what we have to do, all right? Anyway, it's only a temporary thing. We won't stay at the Easton Arms forever. Just a couple of months or so, until I get us on our feet again." She smoothed her skirt. "Now please try to relax about this. I think you're overreacting."

Again, April felt the verbal slap. "Overreacting?"

"Yes." Mom went back to the china cabinet. "This is not the end of the world, you know."

"No," April said. "It's not, Mother. You're right." She tried to keep her voice steady. "Who cares if I made Pep Squad at Covington? Who cares if I don't even get to go to school there anymore, with all my best friends? Who cares if I don't get to go to the Autumn Ball? Right, I'm overreacting. And it's not important that we lost our house, either, is it?" Tears filled her eyes. She fought them away. "Or that we have to live in a bad neighborhood? No, it's not important at all. I'm just *overreacting!*"

By now April was nearly shouting, eyes clouded with tears. Through them she saw Sean with his own eyes wide, half curious and half scared. Ranger's ears stood at full attention.

She tried to lower her voice. "This week has been a

nightmare, Mother. At least you could have warned us. You must have known earlier that this might happen. Why didn't you tell us? This just isn't fair!''

Mom stood at the table, silently holding another dinner plate. She didn't look up or move.

As she watched her mother, April's rage and resentment slowly began to change. Mom's eyes were empty and blank. Her shoulders slumped, giving her that limp look again. April realized her mother was in a daze. She had looked that way all week, as if she were hanging on a thread. A thread that day by day unraveled a little more.

Trembling, April turned and ran upstairs.

''We're going to miss you!'' Andrea sniffled, giving April a big hug Friday night.

It was April's last night in Covington.

Liz Murphy and Dina Stein, two other senior Pep Squad members, hugged her, too. Then Lauren and Toby, standing beside them at the door of Lauren's house, joined in, making April feel enveloped by the caring of her friends.

All around them hung pink party streamers, and on the wall over the snack buffet a banner read GOOD LUCK, APRIL!

''You guys are a great 'pep squad' for me,'' murmured April, pulling away to blow her nose.

The seniors said their good-byes with more hugs, then left. April turned to Toby and Lauren. ''Thanks, you guys. If I'd known going-away parties could be so great, I'd have moved a long time ago!''

Toby grinned. ''I just hope you feel better, instead of worse. I mean, everybody got so mushy.''

''Don't worry. I definitely feel better.'' April laughed. ''A *lot*. Mushy is good for going-away parties. Everyone was terrific. And this cute card from Garrett. I love it!''

''I feel better, too,'' said Lauren, '' 'cause I realized

18

you'll only be thirty minutes away, right? It's not like you're moving to the South Pole or something!''

"Yeah, we're still going to see you a lot," added Toby. "We'll bring you back here for the football games and parties and stuff.''

"My mother said you can spend the night whenever you want," Lauren chimed in. "Even the whole week during vacation time.''

April smiled, putting her arms around her two friends' shoulders. "You two are the *best*. And you know what?''

"What?" Lauren asked.

"You've got the biggest, worst mess since Pompeii on your hands.'' She glanced around at the paper plates and cups and popcorn strewn about. "Do guests of honor have to help clean up?''

"Only if they really, truly care about their absolute best friends," said Toby, pushing out her pudgy lower lip in a fake pout.

They all laughed.

Even after she went home, April kept the party's happy glow with her. It helped to stop thinking about the fact that she was spending her last night in the home she'd known for a decade.

When she opened her eyes the next morning, though, she felt for a moment that she must be somewhere else. Her pretty, comfortable room was gone. In its place were bare walls, empty shelves, and a hollow, echoing silence. Her china doll collection, her grandmother's flower-arrangement paintings, and her old stuffed animals were all packed in boxes downstairs, ready to move. This room would no longer be hers.

For a second, April felt a cold lump of panic in her throat. Then the tears came—only a trickle. She reached for one of the few things left unpacked—a box of tissues—and blew her nose. Then she got up.

About one thing, at least, Mom was right. Today was not the end of the world. Plenty of people had to leave their houses. These days, lots of people lost their homes, just as April's family had. Although she hardly ever read the newspapers, lately she'd begun to look at certain types of articles—the ones about the bad economy and how it was making people default on their home loans.

No matter what happened, it seemed, people just had to pick up and go on. Besides, April thought, her family didn't have it as bad as others. At least Mom still had a job, and a new car, and they had a place to live. Things would get better. Mom had promised they would only have to live in Easton two or three months. Then they could move to a better neighborhood.

In the bathroom mirror, April saw puffy eyes, a red nose, and splotchy pink cheeks. Porky Pig. She'd been looking like him pretty often lately.

To Porky, April whispered, "It's not the end of the world. It's not the end of the world."

After washing, she pulled on the old blue sweater, jeans, and jogging shoes she had laid out the night before. They were the only clothes not packed away. She stripped the bed sheets, then stuffed them and the pillows and fluffy pink comforter into a big plastic bag.

Her soap holder, toothbrush, and comb she dropped into another bag. Taking it and the bag of bed linens, April opened the door. Her fingers touched the light switch, then stopped. Just one more look. She turned and gazed into her room. Then, quickly, she switched off the light.

Chapter 3

The work started right after breakfast. April spent the whole morning with her mother and Sean carrying dozens of boxes from the stacked-up pyramids in the living room to the small moving trailer Mom had rented.

It was hard for April not to think about how the day would have gone if they weren't moving out of their house. Probably there would have been a couple of hours on the phone with Toby or Lauren about hair and clothes for the Autumn Ball that night. Then, in the afternoon, she would have had a long bubble soak in the tub, followed by an hour or so of doing her nails, more time on the phone, then another couple of hours of hair and makeup. Finally, in the evening . . .

"Mo-om," Sean's voice cut in. "Can we stop now?" He sprawled out on top of the few packing boxes left in the living room, prompting Ranger to nuzzle his palm. "It's noon already. We've been moving stuff for *three hours!*"

"Seems more like thirty," April added, joining him on the boxes.

There was nowhere else to sit. Mom had put an ad in the paper and sold the whole living room set to bring in cash for the move. A group of inexpensive student movers from the college had already taken the rest of the downstairs furniture to the apartment. That afternoon they would come for the bedroom pieces.

Mom stood over April and Sean, hands on her hips.

"Looks like mutiny around here. Okay, you two, here's a deal. We load these last few boxes, then stop at Bertie's Big Burgers on the way to the apartment. How's that?"

Sean didn't wait for a second invitation to his favorite restaurant. His energy suddenly returned. He jumped up and shot both fists high in the air. "Big Burgers! All *right!*"

April laughed along with her mother. It was a relief to see Mom back to her old self. The three of them were more or less the same as always now. Underneath the big problems, they were having their little ups and downs, as usual.

After lunch at Bertie's they all got back in the car to heard for the apartment. The moving trailer trundled along behind them. Strange, thought April. It was as if their whole lives had been squeezed into those cardboard boxes riding in the trailer.

Sean was teasing Ranger. "Look, Range, a kitty!" He pointed out his front-seat window.

The dog's ears shot up. He growled and thumped his nose against April's window in the backseat, carefully scoping out passing sidewalks and bushes for cats.

"Stop it, Sean." April stroked the thick black fur on Ranger's back. "He always believes you, poor dog."

"Plus he's leaving nose prints on my windows," Mom complained.

As they crossed the river, the landscape began to change. Warehouses and used-car lots replaced the houses and trees. Then came small factories and long, sprawling office complexes. As they neared the high-rises of downtown, the streets narrowed and trees began to reappear in little corner parks. In one area, tall oaks stood guard in front of stately old Victorian homes. Flowers lined the broad sidewalks, and children played in front yards.

"Is this Easton?" Sean asked. "I like it here."

"No," answered April. "This is Vickers Oaks."

22

"Will there be kids in Easton?" Sean pressed his nose against his window.

"I'm sure you'll find friends at school, honey," Mom told him.

She turned at the city art museum onto a wide boulevard of small boutiques and fancy office buildings. After a few blocks, though, more and more litter began to appear, blowing about on the sidewalks. The buildings looked older and less cared for.

Mom made another turn onto a street that at first looked all brown. On both sides stood four-story walls of brown brick. April realized they were apartment buildings.

Sean read the signs. "Glen Haven Apartments, Richmond Apartments . . ."

"Our building is at 125," Mom said. "Easton Arms."

Tucked in here and there were corner stores and Laundromats. April saw a pawn shop and an optometry store. A flashing red-and-white cola sign advertised a tiny diner.

April's high mood began to sink.

The car stopped. Sean read the sign. "Easton Arms Apartments!"

"Well, here we are," Mom confirmed.

Drawing a deep breath, April followed them out of the car. Ranger, on his leash, stayed at her heels.

Mom stretched, then rubbed the back of her neck. "Want to go up and have a look before we start carrying things in?"

"Yeah!" Sean dashed up the building's front steps. He tried to open the door, but couldn't, settling instead for rattling the doorknob.

"Honey, wait," Mom said. "You need a key for the main door. It's for security."

"Cool!" Sean grinned happily. "But how will we know when our friends come over?"

"There's a doorbell here for each apartment. See?" Mom pointed at the wall beside the door. "If someone rings our bell, we can let them in by pushing a special button in our apartment."

"Really? *Cool!*" He pressed the bell for number 416. "I'm the first person to ring our doorbell!"

April smiled. The idea of living in the Easton Arms certainly didn't seem to bother Sean. The second Mom unlocked the door, he raced ahead upstairs.

"It's on the fourth floor," Mom called. Then she turned to April. "There's an elevator, too, right there. Do you want to use it?"

April shook her head. "The stairs are fine."

Ranger led the way after Sean. He sniffed everything, ears up, investigating.

April, on the other hand, held her breath with every step up the dark, narrow stairwell. A powerful, fake-flower smell doused the air, as if someone had emptied a whole can of air freshener. Then, farther up the stairs, the smell turned musty.

Mom read her mind. "It's this carpet. Awfully old. Needs a good cleaning."

Reaching the fourth floor, they heard Sean running down the hall. "Here it is!"

Mom took out another key. At number 416, they all stopped, waiting for her to unlock it.

"This is it, folks," she said, finally pushing the door open.

Ranger charged in behind Sean. April entered next, stopping just inside the door. She didn't want to go further.

The carpet was the color of old green bubble gum, mottled by stains that looked as if someone had given a car an oil change right in the living room. Green curtains on the windows hung torn and tattered. Smudges and greasy hand prints decorated the walls. Maybe a car mechanic had lived there.

"It's a mess," Mom said. "I know."

April stuffed her hands further into her pockets. She felt cold, even though the room was hot and stuffy. "Didn't the manager clean it after the last renters left?"

Sean pulled back the curtains to look out on the street. "Hey, neat! You can see the whole street!" He dashed down a short hall toward the bedrooms.

"She was supposed to," said Mom, "but I negotiated with her to give us half the first month's rent off in exchange for cleaning it ourselves."

A few moments later Sean emerged from the kitchen. "Hey, come look. There's this weird-looking thing in here. What is it—some kind of dishwasher?"

Mom laughed. "You must be looking at the radiator, honey. There is no dishwasher. Look at this kitchen, though. There's plenty of space. Eventually we can get one of those hook-up dishwashers."

Eventually. The word rolled around in April's mind. Watching her mother pluck a wadded-up paper towel from the countertop, she suddenly realized what the word meant. Mom had promised they'd stay at Easton Arms for only a couple of months, but the truth was, they were going to have to live there much, much longer.

April sat at the kitchen table, making a grocery list. It was Sunday morning, not even a whole day since they'd moved into the apartment, and already Mom stood on a stepladder painting the kitchen walls bright sunflower-yellow.

"Potato chips," said Sean. "We need potato chips." He stood at the sink, scrubbing the refrigerator rack Mom had set him to work on.

"Okay, potato chips." April added it to her list under milk, eggs, bread, and bug spray.

Last night had brought a big surprise—and not a pleasant one. Cockroaches a big as April's thumb, black

25

and shiny, had scurried all over the kitchen countertops when she came in at bedtime for a glass of water. Growing up in Covington, April had seen a total of three or four roaches in her whole life. Never a whole army of them!

"How about if *I* go to the store and *April* cleans the refrigerator?" Sean proposed hopefully.

Mom raised an eyebrow with a small grin. "Stop complaining. You've already conned me into an allowance increase for this. Better quit while you're ahead."

"Do I get an allowance increase, too?" April ventured. The amount of her own allowance had dwindled drastically in recent months.

"Hey, yours is already three times more than mine!" Sean objected.

Mom adjusted the pink bandana covering her hair. "For going to the corner store? Hmm. Clean the bathroom when you get back and your chances look good."

April finished the list and put the twenty-dollar bill Mom had given her in her jeans pocket. "See you later, you two. Have fun."

"Yeah, a real blast," Sean muttered.

Mom laughed. "Nothing like a little enthusiasm."

April left smiling. Things really did seem back to normal. If she ignored the fact that she and her family were living in a crummy apartment, in Easton, with roaches, life really wasn't too different from before. That is, if she also ignored having to give up the Pep Squad, going to the dance with Garrett Martin . . . She made herself stop.

On the way down the block to the store, April thought instead about Langley High, where she'd start tomorrow. She didn't even know where it was, much less what it was like. All she knew was what she'd heard. It sat right in the middle of one of the city's roughest neighborhoods, had state champion sports teams, and good drama and debate teams.

Tomorrow she'd be a new kid at Langley, starting the semester a month late, not knowing a soul. The idea made her queasy. She tried not to think about it. Instead, she glanced around her.

People hurried past in all directions. Others stood in small groups on the front stoops of apartment houses, or sat on the steps. Wilcox Avenue was as busy as the Covington shopping mall—nothing like the quiet residential streets April was used to.

She passed a bunch of children playing hopscotch on the sidewalk, watched by a pair of grandmothers in lawn chairs. Farther down, in front of the store, a knot of young men chanted along with a rap song playing on a boom box.

Just as April was turning into the store a voice called out, "Hey, where you goin', beautiful?"

She half-turned and saw one of the men, a blond in army camouflage fatigues, whistling at her. "Come back, babe!"

She turned away quickly.

"Hey, what's the matter? Can't even say hello?" growled another.

A stinging blush rose to April's cheeks. She hurried into the store. For a moment she just stood near the entrance, completely rattled. Slipping her hand into her pocket, she found the list. Like a protective charm, it calmed her. She grabbed a plastic shopping basket.

After paying for her groceries, she walked slowly to the door and looked out. The men were still there on the sidewalk. She took a deep breath. The way they had talked to her made her angry. It frightened her, too. The thought of walking past them again made her knees wobble.

"Those good-for-nothin's give you a hard time?" the elderly woman at the cash register asked.

April shrugged nervously and nodded.

The woman frowned behind her thick glasses. Her

27

white hair was sprayed into a permanent helmet shape. "Don't pay attention to 'em. Just ignore 'em."

"I'm trying," said April, "but . . ."

The woman nodded. "Yeah, I know. Tell you what. Go out my side door there. Where are you headed?"

"That way on Wilcox." April pointed. "Past *them.*"

The woman smiled, showing a gold front tooth. "Then just go out that side door to Turner Boulevard, cross at the corner, cross Wilcox at the other corner—"

"And walk up the opposite side of the street?" April finished.

"You got it." The woman winked. "Anyway, I'm gonna see if I can get the cops out here to chase those losers away. They're loitering."

April nodded, thanked the woman again, and took the escape route across Turner Boulevard.

The men were too busy harassing other women to notice her so far away. Relieved, April started up the opposite side of Wilcox.

At first glance it looked just like the Easton Arms side: a solid wall of brown buildings, fronted by high stoops, wide stairs, and an occasional skinny elm tree. The sidewalk was just as crowded, too.

April tried to keep her eyes on the pavement this time, afraid of encountering another group like the one outside the store. But after a moment, what she saw on the pavement worried her even more.

A small, dark-haired woman about Mom's age lay on the ground, curled on her side in a tight little ball.

"Oh!" April gasped.

The woman's skin was pale, almost gray—the color of a fogged sky. Eyes shut tight, she moaned.

April stared in horror, unsure of what to do.

"Keep away from her." Another woman shuffled up out of nowhere to chase off the gathering crowd. "I called the cops already, okay? Keep clear." The shuffling woman's eyes looked dull and glassy in a puffed, swollen face. Her gray-streaked hair hung in greasy strings about her shoulders.

Nausea turned April's stomach. She hurried away, hugging the grocery bag tight as she ran down the street. Finally, panting, she slowed and shut her eyes. Maybe when she opened them she'd be back on her own clean, pretty street in Covington. But that didn't happen.

When April opened her eyes she saw a very young woman sitting on the bottom step of an apartment building, nursing a baby. A dusty-looking toddler leaned against her, sucking his thumb. As April passed, the woman held out her palm.

"I can't buy milk," she murmured, so softly April barely heard.

"I—I'm sorry," April whispered back. There was milk in the grocery bag. There was change in her pocket. But she felt frozen. No one had ever begged her for money before. No one begged in Covington.

Slowly, the woman dropped her hand and used it to rearrange the thin blanket covering her baby.

April walked on. She crossed the street to the Easton Arms and climbed the stairs. It wasn't until she took out her keys at the door of the apartment that she realized she was shaking.

Chapter 4

April shut the door behind her, still trembling. Slowly, she set the bag of groceries on the floor and turned to lock the door. It had a knob lock, bar, and a chain. She slid all three into place, hoping somehow to shut herself away from Wilcox Avenue.

But she couldn't. In her mind reeled images of the men whistling at her and the gray face of the woman curled up on the sidewalk and the young mother's outstretched palm.

Leaning against the door, April drew a breath. She felt Ranger's warm muzzle in her palm. His brown eyes looked up at her questioningly.

"It's all right, Range," she whispered. "I'm okay."

The gentle nudge of his shoulder against her leg and the soft touch of his fur calmed her enough so that she could pick up the bag of groceries.

"Oh, here she is," said Mom as April entered the kitchen. "We were beginning to think you had taken our money and run." She turned and smiled at April—looked right at her—and saw nothing.

Her mother didn't notice anything at all wrong with April. It was as if her walk down Wilcox and back had never happened. Every minute of it was burned into April's brain, but Mom had no idea.

All the fear and confusion of that walk and of the whole past week began tumbling inside her. She stared at the back of her mother's head as she continued painting, and felt a hard, biting anger.

How could Mom close her eyes to what was happening? Those people in the street—those miserable, ragged people—most of them had once had places to live and food on their tables, too. Probably not very long ago. April remembered the newspaper articles about homelessness. They talked about how easy it was to lose everything—how you could end up on the street before you even knew it was happening.

April set the grocery bag on the table. Sean rushed for the potato chips, and Mom told him he couldn't have any until lunch. Just an hour ago, that kind of normal conversation would have made April feel better about

30

their move to Easton. Now, though, there was a thick knot in her chest. It was like being on the slow part of a roller coaster, when things seem perfectly smooth and safe, but you know that in just seconds you're going to plunge over the edge into a long, screaming drop.

"Did you find low-fat milk?" Mom wiped her brush on the rim of the paint can.

April nodded.

"Good. Thanks. We'll have tomato soup and omelettes for lunch. How does this color look, sweetheart, now that I've got a whole wall done?" Mom climbed off the ladder and stood back, hands on hips, head tilted.

The bubbly cheer in her voice only hardened the knot in April's chest. Mom seemed determined to turn the apartment into something you'd see in Covington, instead of Easton.

"Well, what do you think?" Mom repeated, looking at her.

"It's fine," said April. She kept her eyes on the carton of eggs she was unloading from the bag. "Looks fine."

She knew Mom wanted to make the apartment a home for the three of them. But just how much stood between them and those people on the street? What if this home didn't last, either?

The building was dark. Fluorescent fixtures dimly lit the high-ceilinged entryway. The halls had scuffed gray linoleum floors and dull beige walls. Even from the outside, when her school bus had driven up to the entrance, Langley High had looked depressing to April. Big and square, it had tiny windows peeking out through the gray stone front wall.

The place couldn't have been more different from Covington High. According to a brass plaque April had spotted on Langley's outside wall, it was the oldest public high school in the state. A historical landmark. And it looked like it—positively ancient.

She walked down the hall looking for her locker, number 656. Her stomach felt a little nervous, but not as bad as she'd expected. While waiting for the bus that morning she'd given herself a pep talk. All schools got new students every year. No way would she be the only new kid at Langley. Plus, she'd never had trouble making friends before. Why should it be any harder here?

True, the kids on the bus had seemed pretty different from people at Covington. A lot of them wore black—leather jackets, high-top sneakers, black jeans—with hair teased half a foot tall, and six or seven earrings apiece on girls *and* boys. Heavy-metal types. Maybe that was the look for Easton, April decided. And it was exactly what made her stand out like a sore thumb.

She had worn her best jeans and sweater, suede boots, gold hoop earrings and had moussed her hair into fluffy blond waves. At Covington, that would be the best look for the first day of school.

At Langley, though, it seemed all wrong. In the halls were more kids dressed like the ones on the bus. There were also guys with the skater look, with long hair, long shorts, and Hawaiian shirts, then a few nerdy types with pocket protectors, and some Madonna-clone girls.

April felt like an ant from a different hill. The only good thing was that no one seemed to notice. A few people glanced in her direction, but no one looked twice.

That was a relief. For the time being, she didn't mind being ignored. All she wanted was to take things in. She began to forget about the depressing building, feeling instead a quiet, rumbling excitement. The air around her seemed to buzz. There was so much going on—kids talking, laughing, singing, yelling—all kinds of kids. At Covington, everyone had looked more or less the same, talked the same, acted the same. Compared to Langley, Covington had been like a plain bowl of oatmeal.

Finally April spotted the rows of 600s lockers. The lockers were the one thing about Langley identical to

Covington. That same mouse-brown color. All school lockers in the universe probably came from the same factory somewhere, April decided. A small smile played on her lips as she hung her brown suede jacket on the hook inside. The gesture made her feel secure, as if she belonged at Langley just a little bit more.

"Who are you?" A short girl two lockers away smiled at her. Her black hair stood out in a close-cropped burr on the sides. A long, glossy sheaf from the top draped over one eye.

"Oh, hi. I'm April Morgan, a new sophomore."

The girl nodded. "I'm Yoko Rodriguez, old sophomore." She wore a blue mechanic's jumpsuit with a dozen different necklaces made of beads and seashells and knotted yarn.

April's eyes settled on the name patch stitched on the jumpsuit's breast pocket, just like a gas-station attendant's. "Yoko?" she repeated.

"Yeah." The girl stopped smiling. "Japanese. Short for Kyoko. So what?" She smacked her chewing gum and held out a pack to April. "Want some?"

April shook her head. "No thanks."

Yoko narrowed her eyes and aimed them at April's sweater and jeans, then back up to her hair and makeup. "Miss Teenage America, huh? What's wrong? Afraid my gum is laced with drugs or something?" She gave a short laugh, then walked away.

April just stood there, mouth open. What had she done to deserve *that?*

Before she could recover, she felt a hard, thudding blow that pushed her backward against her locker. Somebody had plowed into her. Just as quickly, he straightened out and scurried away toward the group of boys surrounding them.

"Hey, you scored, Mick! All *right!*" one of them whooped.

33

"Always had a way with the ladies, didn't you?" another one shouted, shoving Mick again.

April jumped out of the way just in time, banging her elbow on another locker. Half dazed, she stared at the boys. Some of them wore white T-shirts tucked into cuffed jeans. Others wore wide black leather belts hung with chains. But they all had razor-short hair and tattoos of dragons on their arms.

Skinheads, April realized with a shudder. She had seen people like them on the television news, waving Nazi flags.

She didn't wait another minute. She hurried away down the hall.

"Aw, we scared the little girl," raspy voices called after her.

It was all she could do not to break into a run.

"Well, how was it?"

On the phone that afternoon, Toby's voice was like a long, cool drink of water. April settled back against her bed pillows, trying to figure out how to answer.

Even before her first class at Langley she had been insulted, pushed around, and driven to the brink of tears. After escaping the skinheads, she'd had to hide in the rest room to fight off the tears, which had made her late to homeroom on top of everything else. She'd have given anything to be able to run home, to her *real* home in Covington, where she belonged.

"It was okay," she told Toby.

"Don't get too enthusiastic, now." Toby laughed in her big, hearty way.

That sound brought April near tears again. She missed Toby's laugh. She missed sitting with her friends in class and hanging around with them in the halls and at lunch. The worst thing about Langley so far wasn't Yoko Rodriguez or the skinheads. The worst thing was being alone.

34

"When can we come over?" Toby asked. "Lauren was wondering about Saturday."

"Here?" April bit her bottom lip.

"No—the Washington Monument. Of course *there*. That's how it works when one friend can drive and the other can't, you know. I'm sixteen, you're not."

"Well, I—"

"And don't tell me your family is still too busy unpacking. You could have unpacked six large tribes by now."

"We're through, but . . . we're still cleaning and stuff, and . . ." April shut her eyes. She didn't want to lie. "I can't really have company."

It wasn't a lie. She still wasn't ready to let any of her Covington friends see the apartment. It was so, so different from her pretty house in Covington, and from all of their beautiful homes.

"All right. But just say the word when you're no longer too busy for us, Your Royal Highness." Toby sighed. "Boy, this thirty-minute distance between Easton and Covington is beginning to seem like half a world, right?"

April nodded. "A *whole* world."

On the school bus the next morning she gave herself another pep talk. Her first day at Langley hadn't gone very well, to say the least, but maybe she had just happened on the wrong people. And maybe her clothes had been too conspicuous. That Yoko girl's crack about Miss Teenage America had really stung. Today she had tucked a plaid flannel shirt into a pair of jeans, slipped on some loafers, and toned down her hair and makeup.

It was time to get busy. There had to be friendly kids at Langley, somewhere.

At least the teachers seemed friendly. After homeroom April asked Ms. Reynolds about the school's cheerleading team. The teacher said the cheerleaders' election had already taken place, but suggested April visit the gym during the activities period after lunch to watch a practice of the Langley Sparklers, the drill team.

On a bench outsid the cafeteria, April hurried through her sandwich. She checked her school map again for the gym. The day before, it had taken her forever to find her P.E. class.

Her heart beat a little faster as she walked beside the tennis courts toward the gym. The excitement of her summer Pep Squad workouts with Lauren and Andrea started pumping back in. There was something really thrilling about the snappy, quick steps, and the idea of performing for roaring audiences at big games.

From halfway across the soccer field, April heard music. It was a jazzy popular tune with a deep drumbeat. She quickened her pace to match it. Soon she stood in the open doorway of the gym, but for a moment she wondered if she had taken a wrong turn somewhere.

About fifty kids crowded the gym floor, leaping, stomping, and singing. They wore colorful leotards and tights, hair pulled back, faces sweaty and flushed. Amazingly, there were girls *and* boys. Could this be the Sparklers? These people looked more like Olympic gymnasts and Broadway dancers than a high-school drill team. April's heart sank.

"Need something?" asked a short, muscular man striding toward her.

"Oh, I, um, was looking for the Sparklers."

"That's us," he said, smiling. "I'm Mr. Greer, the director. How can I help you?"

"Well . . . I just started school here yesterday, and I wondered—"

"You were interested in trying out?" Mr. Greer scrunched up half of his heavily tanned face. "Hmm. Sorry, but I'm going to be honest with you. I'm not looking for new Sparklers. Most of these kids have been working on our routines since last year, and the rest for the past month."

"I've got some experience," April interrupted. She smiled. "I was elected to the Covington High Pep Squad, but my family had to move . . ."

Mr. Greer shook his head sympathetically. "Bum break. I bet you're good, too. You've got some Sparkler in you, I can tell. Great smile. And not a giver-upper, are you? That's terrific. But listen, I'm really sorry. If I had even one space I'd give you a whack at it. You've just come in too late this semester."

"Is that final?" April asked. "You're absolutely sure?"

Mr. Greer chuckled softly. "I'm absolutely sure. But know what? I'm not worried about you. Like I said, you're no giver-upper. Somewhere here at Langley, I'm going to hear you making a big splash."

April couldn't help joining him in a laugh. If only getting rejected were always this friendly.

Mr. Greer went back to his team and clapped out a new rhythm. For a moment, April watched from the doorway, expecting to feel down and depressed, or at least jealous. To her surprise, what she felt was relieved.

To win a spot on the Covington Pep Squad, all you had to do was be a girl, be popular or at least well-liked, and learn a few cheers. Being cute couldn't hurt, either. If you were sort of athletic, your chances were even better. But no one expected you to dance like Paula Abdul, or, for heaven's sake, *sing!*

April knew she couldn't just waltz in on a team like the Sparklers and catch up. At the moment, she didn't have the skills. The problem was, she couldn't think of any skills she *did* have, besides her pretty smile.

Mr. Greer's prediction that she'd make a splash somewhere at Langley echoed in her head. But while walking to her next class, passing crowds of kids who were absolutely nothing like her, April had her doubts. A big splash? She couldn't even find a place to dive in.

Chapter 5

"Ms. Morgan, would you read for us this passage from the Declaration of Independence?"

April's history teacher, Mr. Wortham, sat on a corner of his desk Wednesday afternoon, gazing over the tops of his wire-rim glasses at her.

"Stand, please," he drawled in his Southern accent. With dark skin, salt-and-pepper hair, and a portly frame, he reminded April of James Earl Jones.

Her stomach knotted. The last thing she wanted that day was to be the center of attention. It was her third day at Langley, and the only good thing about it so far was that no more skinheads or Yoko Rodriguez types had hassled her, and no other clubs or teams had turned her down.

Of course, she hadn't tried to join any, either. Nor had she tried to talk to anyone. Mostly April just wanted to keep her head above water. At the moment that was hard enough.

"Um, where should I start?" she asked.

"The beginning's always a good place." Mr. Wortham chuckled.

Some of the kids laughed.

The knot in April's stomach twisted. Slowly, she rose from her seat. Why couldn't Mr. Wortham pick on someone else?

She looked down at the textbook on her desk, clearing her throat.

"Why don't you hold the text in your hands?" the teacher suggested. "It's easier to read that way."

April held the book at waist-level, stealing a glance out at the class. A lot of people were talking, doodling in their notebooks, or otherwise paying little attention. That made her feel better.

She cleared her throat again. " 'We hold these truths to be self-evident—' "

"Higher," said Mr. Wortham.

April looked up. "Pardon me?"

"Your text—hold it higher, and keep your head higher, so that your voice won't be stuck in your throat like a frog in a barrel." He did an exaggerated imitation of how she'd been reading, pressing his chin against his throat and pretending to gag.

April couldn't help blushing, half in embarrassment, half in annoyance with the teacher. She remembered having heard that he coached the school Speech and Drama League. He probably couldn't help correcting people's reading styles. Someone else used to correct her, too—her father, who always helped her learn her lines for grade-school plays.

Open your voice, April, Dad used to say. *Pretend your audience is shivering with cold, and your voice is going to warm them up.*

April took a breath and began again. " 'We hold these truths to be self-evident . . .' "

What are you trying to say? Dad asked in her head. *Think about what your lines mean.* Dad, a public-relations consultant, made his living knowing how to talk.

" ' . . . that all men are created equal . . .' " April slowed on the words. They were beautiful, and more than just words. She focused on the ideas behind them. " ' . . . that they were endowed by their Creator with certain unalienable rights . . .' " After a pause, she began softly on the next line. " ' . . . that among these

39

are life, liberty and the pursuit of happiness.' '' Slowly her voice rose. In her mind was the fact that countless people's lives and whole nations had changed because of the words she was reading.

'' 'That to secure these rights . . .' '' She paused again. '' ' . . . governments are instituted among men, deriving their just powers from the consent of the governed . . .' '' She took a breath. '' ' . . . that whenever any form of government becomes destructive of these ends, it is the right of the people to alter or abolish it, and to institute new government.' ''

When April finished, she looked up. The whole class sat silent, staring at her.

Great, she thought. Along with "Miss Teenage America" and "Little Girl," now they'd be calling her "George" or "Tom Jefferson."

The school bell rang. She sat down and gathered her books quickly, hoping to make it out the door before anyone said anything. But she had just stood up again when Mr. Wortham called, "Ms. Morgan, may I see you for a moment?"

He gazed at her over the tops of his glasses again, very seriously.

As she approached he asked, "Have you got lots of clubs and school activities lined up yet this semester?"

April frowned. Was he trying to be funny? "I wouldn't say that," she answered. "I just started here three days ago."

"I know." Mr. Wortham crossed his arms. "That's why I'm hoping you'll consider an activity in which I think you'd be very good. Heard of the Langley Speech and Drama League?"

"Yes, but I've never—"

"Experience not required," the teacher interrupted. "You've got talent. That was a good reading you gave today."

"Really?"

40

"Bordering on excellent, I'd say." Mr. Wortham nodded. "Our next meeting is today during activities period after lunch, right here. Why don't you drop by?"

April felt the heaviness in her stomach lighten and start to float away. In fact, she felt light all over—almost giddy. This was the first good thing that had happened all week.

She smiled. "Thanks. I'll be here."

The Langley Speech and Drama League had a reputation. At Covington April had heard people talk in hushed, respectful tones about upcoming tournaments against Langley.

On first glance at the Langley League that afternoon, though, she never would have guessed that anyone would fear them. Her first impressions were that she had come to the wrong room, and that three clubs were about to meet there, instead of one. In one corner, total chaos reigned: kids laughing, throwing paper wads at each other, switching desks around. In the opposite corner people bent diligently over their textbooks or just sat quietly.

The back of the room looked like girls-only territory. For a moment she wondered if she was in Covington again. The girls in the back wore great clothes, neatly styled hair, and pretty makeup. Any one of them could have been a Pep Squad member. April had thought there was no one at all like her at Langley—let alone a whole group!

She wanted to meet them. As she approached the group of girls she noticed there were no empty chairs nearby. They sat a bit apart from everyone else, pulled away into a tight circle.

When April finally found a chair, it was nowhere near the girls, but at least it sat safely out of the line of paper-wad fire. The kids around her were the quiet ones. One

41

of them, a boy with light-brown hair and glasses, was looking at her.

"Hi," she said.

The boy answered, "Hi."

April slipped out of her jacket and hung it over the back of her chair.

"I haven't seen you here before, have I?" asked the boy.

"Probably not, considering I haven't been here before." April smiled.

He crossed his blue eyes, making a funny face. "That sounds logical." He thrust his hand forward. "Mason Doherty, by the way."

"Oh. April Morgan." She took his hand and they shook.

Mason nodded. "You're in my trig class, aren't you?"

"Oh, yeah. I thought you looked familiar. Did you survive the pop quiz?"

"Barely." Mason rolled his eyes. "That was a killer."

April laughed. "I'm not going to think about it."

"In that case, tell me why you decided to do something so insane as to join us here today."

"You mean the Speech and Drama League?"

Mason nodded. "The S.D.L. Society for the Deranged and Lackluster."

"Lackluster?" April shook her head. "That's not what I've heard."

"We put up a good front. Anyhow, are you signing up?"

"I don't know." April shrugged. "I've never done anything like this. I just thought I'd come and see . . ."

"And so far you're really impressed, right?" Mason gestured toward the groups around them. "I mean, we've got the Nerds, the Heathen, and the Gee Gees."

"Gee Gees?" April repeated.

"Glamour Girls."

April grinned. "You're terrible!"

42

"Don't tell me you hadn't noticed them." Mason jerked his head toward the Covington lookalikes.

"Well . . ." April bit her lip, trying to stop laughing. "The differences within this room *are* pretty noticeable."

"For some reason we all work pretty well together anyway. Amazing, when you think about it. Oh, here comes Wortham."

The room quieted as the teacher strode to the front desk. He began the meeting with an announcement about an upcoming tournament, then turned things over to the S.D.L. president, a tall, blond girl who had been sitting with the Gee Gees. She talked about the club budget and setting up car-pool rides to the tournament.

During the last part of the hour Mr. Wortham led everyone in voice exercises that April was sure could be heard across the street. He also read to them a collection of quotes from famous authors about "projecting" your voice and emotions.

At the end, he came over and gave April a folder of information about the League. "Let me know next week if you've decided to join."

"Well?" asked Mason as they walked out to the hall together. "What do you think?"

Leafing through the information the teacher had given her, April shrugged. "Like I said, I've never been in a speech and drama group before."

"Neither had anyone else before they joined, right?" Mason pointed out.

April smiled at him. It occurred to her that she was making her first friend at Langley. Mason was so easygoing and pleasant that she had felt comfortable with him right away.

And he was right about joining. Everyone had to start somewhere.

She remembered how involved and even powerful she

43

had felt while reading the passage from the Declaration of Independence for Mr. Wortham's history class.

Maybe the S.D.L. was her place to dive in.

"I'll cut some tomatoes for the salad," April told her mother one night early the following week as they made dinner together.

Sean was at soccer practice. He seemed to be doing fine at his new school. Being good at soccer had won him instant status with the other fourth-grade boys.

"We don't have any tomatoes, sweetheart," Mom said, stirring a pot of stew.

April peered into the refrigerator. "You sure? They were on the list you took to the store yesterday."

"I didn't get them," Mom said.

"Why not?"

"The price has jumped sky-high because of that early freeze."

"Oh." April looked in the vegetable drawer. Nothing was there. "You didn't get any vegetables?"

"Lettuce and carrots." Mom pointed at the bags on the counter.

"That's not enough for all our dinners this week. And you only got a half gallon of milk."

"That's all I could get, April."

She looked at her mother.

"Shut the fridge door, sweetheart. You're letting the cold out." Mom sounded normal, but a deep frown was etched on her forehead. "We're on a very tight budget. You know that."

"It's never been so tight you couldn't buy food."

Mom went on stirring the stew. "I had twenty-five dollars to shop with yesterday. It's all I'll have until Wednesday, my payday."

"You can't buy more groceries until Wednesday?" April's eyes widened.

Mom nodded. "Today I had to pay rent to Mrs. Kriss.

This week I had to pay the utilities and the car loan. That didn't leave much.''

April sat down at the kitchen table.

"Sweetheart, you don't have to get so upset about this. We have plenty of food in the house. I have a meal plan worked out. We won't go hungry.'' Holding the spoon in one hand, Mom walked over and gave April a one-armed hug. "I promise.''

April looked up, hoping to find the answers to all her questions in her mother's eyes. But all she found was Mom's smile, the same one she had been wearing for days.

While April was doing her homework later that evening, Toby called.

"I'm not letting you off the hook this time,'' Toby warned a couple of minutes into the conversation. "You're coming to Andrea's party if I have to drag you to it.''

April smiled. "Hold your horses. I didn't say I wouldn't go.''

"Yeah, but you had that whiny sound in your voice that you get when you're about to make excuses. I mean, Lauren and I are starting to believe that Langley must be really great. You never want to come back and see us Covington folks anymore. You must have a million new friends keeping you busy.''

April snorted. "Right. They're stampeding to my door. Of *course* I want to see you guys, Toby. It's just that—''

"Oh, no. The whiny sound. I thought you said you'd come.''

"No, I didn't say that, but . . .'' April bit her lip. She couldn't hide in the Easton Arms forever. Sooner or later her friends would have to see the apartment and discover what was happening in her life. She sighed. "I'd like to come. Thanks, Toby. I mean, for always inviting me to things. I really do miss you guys—a *lot.*''

"Is that a 'yes'? I'll be there at seven Saturday night to get you, okay? Lauren can't come with me 'cause she'll be helping Andrea set up, but she said to tell you that if you don't come she'll personally come over there and strangle you. Besides, Wilsey wants you to bring your tapes."

April laughed. "I guess I'd better show up, then."

Saturday night, the minute she and Toby walked into Andrea's house, April regretted not having come back to visit in Covington a lot sooner. A swarm of her friends surrounded her.

"April! Hey, April's here! Hi, April!"

Voices all around asked how she had been and why she had stayed away so long. It was as if she could fit right back into the crowd—as if she had never left.

In the kitchen, Andrea handed April a can of strawberry soda, her favorite. "People at school always talk about how much they miss you."

Lauren nodded. "I hear it all the time, too."

"So do I," added Wilsey. "From the guys, even."

April giggled.

Wilsey leaned closer and whispered, "Jake says the football-team guys are sorry they don't get to watch you on the Pep Squad."

"Oh, Wilsey!" April gave her a little shove.

"She's right," said Toby. "Every guy at school went bug-eyed when you got elected."

April shook her head. Her friends were being goofy, but she didn't mind at all. It was great just to be with them again. "Is Garrett coming tonight?"

Everyone went quiet.

"He's coming late," Andrea finally said, "and . . ."

Lauren grimaced. "He's bringing Becky Keaton."

"Oh." April shrugged.

"Andrea just told me about it today," said Toby apologetically. "I would have told you, but—"

"It's no big deal." April concentrated on keeping her

46

voice even. Something like a little stab caught her in the vicinity of her heart. She had wondered why Garrett never tried to call or at least send a message through Toby or Lauren. "We weren't even dating."

"Yeah, you weren't dating, but—" Wilsey began, then shrugged.

"Hey, you guys." April made herself smile widely. "I am not in love with Garrett Martin, okay? At least, no more than any of *you* are." She poked each of her friends in the ribs until they all started laughing with her. The last thing she wanted was for anyone to feel sorry for her.

She hadn't really been *in love* with Garrett, anyway. It was a crush, mixed with excitement about someone as cute and popular as Garrett being interested in her. She certainly didn't expect him to chase her across town to Easton. Still, there was that little pang in her chest.

More than hurt, she felt angry. The reason why Garrett had never called her again became very clear. Apparently, he had certain requirements for girlfriends. Becky Keaton was a Covington Pep Squad member, cute and popular. April no longer fulfilled all three of those requirements. Dating someone from Easton just didn't fit into Garrett Martin's picture.

After a while Andrea put on a new tape in the den, and everyone started dancing. April got lost in the deep, dreamy beat of the music. Carl Cowles, the first boy she'd ever dated back in eighth grade, asked her to dance. So did several other guys. For the first time in two weeks April began to feel happy.

It really seemed as if nothing at all had changed. Some sort of time warp had slipped her right back to where she had been before Mom's big announcement.

An hour later she left the den to get something to drink. In the kitchen she found Jenette Wright, Patti Berg, and some other Pep Squad girls.

"Hi," she said, fanning herself. "Why aren't you guys dancing?"

"Dancing? I never want to dance again," Patti moaned. "We had practice all afternoon."

Regina Azadian nodded. "You should be glad you didn't get to be on the Pep Squad, April. It is going to be so much work this year!"

"Perkins is a slave driver," said Dina Stein.

"Who's Perkins?" April asked.

"Ms. Perkins, our new coach," explained Jenette. "Didn't you hear? Ms. Whitehurst quit a couple of weeks ago. Right after you left, I guess."

"Oh." April nodded.

"Did you get that routine we practiced today?" Patti asked no one in particular, high-stepping across the kitchen.

Jenette joined her.

"Who knows where Perkins dug up *this* one." Liz Murphy set her can of soda on the countertop and stepped out alongside the others.

"It's so old-fashioned," agreed Regina.

"And if we don't know it by next week," Jenette huffed between jumps, "she'll make us do ten extra sit-ups during warm-ups."

The whole group fell into formation, heels clicking in rhythm on the shiny floor tile.

So much for being tired of dancing, April thought.

The girls stopped now and then to correct mistakes or repeat difficult sequences, but they remained totally engrossed in the routine and in working together. They giggled, they teased, and they taught each other. Great friends; a team.

April might as well not have been there. The Pep Squad girls had forgotten all about her. And why shouldn't they? She wasn't on the squad. She didn't know the routines. She didn't even know about Ms. Perkins.

The kitchen door swung open.

"Oh, there you are, April." Lauren blew upwards at her auburn bangs. "Help me make more popcorn, okay? It's going fast."

April held the popcorn machine lid open while Lauren scooped in the kernels.

"Am I missing a practice here?" Lauren asked the other girls.

In the middle of a sideways chassé step, Liz nodded and waved her over. "Come on, Lauren."

"Can't." Lauren shook her head. "Somebody's got to act responsible while Andrea's dancing with Kirk Bushnell."

"Oh, come on," Jenette urged. "You're the only one who really got this routine."

"Go on, Lauren. I can handle the popcorn," April offered.

"Well . . ." Lauren shrugged. "Okay. Thanks."

April listened as Lauren barked out the steps for the routine. When the corn was all popped she poured it into the bowl, mixed in the butter and spices, then carried it out to the living room, giving one last look over her shoulder at the Pep Squad girls.

"All *right!* More food!" Craig Hensen dug a fist into the bowl before April had a chance to set it on the coffee table. A few kernels landed on the Shetland sweater draped over his broad shoulders. He brushed them off to the rug.

"Way to go, April," said Leonard Maas, stuffing his own mouth full. "Great popcorn." As his hand moved, the gold I.D. bracelet on his wrist caught the light.

"See, everybody's glad you're back." Wilsey walked up and winked.

"All I have to do is make popcorn to stay popular, huh?" April laughed. "That's easy."

"What's it like over there at Langley, anyway?" asked Craig, inhaling another fistful of popcorn. "Tough place?"

49

"Aren't you terrified, going there?" Wilsey wrinkled her nose. "It's so . . . inner-city."

"Yeah, and you don't have men like us around to protect you, like Covington girls do." Leonard slipped an arm around Wilsey. The two of them looked like teammates, wearing identical blue silk sports jackets.

"Men?" Wilsey snickered. "Got any more jokes?" But she was blushing and gazing up at Leonard with a little smile.

"Hey, you females just aren't grateful," Craig mumbled through a mouthful of popcorn.

The realization hit April with a jolt. Wilsey and Leonard. The smiles, the matching jackets . . . A couple? When had *that* happened?

"Hey, you're wearing them, aren't you?" said Leonard as he pushed a strand of hair behind Wilsey's ear.

"My earrings? Of course I am. Look what Leonard gave me, April."

Two small diamond studs sparkled on either side of Wilsey's heart-shaped face.

"And look what I gave him." Wilsey pointed at Leonard's wrist.

April nodded at the sparkle of the diamonds and the gleam of the gold bracelet. Leonard and Wilsey themselves seemed to sparkle and gleam. They made a good-looking couple—a tall, blond boy and a dark, petite girl, both happy and well-scrubbed, like a real-life Ken and Barbie.

As her gaze wandered the room, April realized that was how almost everyone there looked. Clean, well-dressed, even kind of rich. Lots of ski sweaters and expensive sneakers. It had always been that way in Covington. She had just never noticed before.

It was different from Easton. Very different.

Craig moved his feet and fists into a karate stance. He started taking soft shots at Leonard. In a minute they were play-sparring around the room.

50

"Careful!" shrieked Wilsey. "You're going to break something!"

The boys nearly crashed into a big bronze sculpture of a fish on the side table. They set the Persian rug askew, then leaped over the leather sofa, knocking off tapestry pillows in their wake.

April dove for the popcorn bowl just in time. She moved it to the dining room.

"Hi, April," Melissa James called.

"Well, hi!" April smiled back at Melissa and her friends Terri Krieg and Susan Markum. "Did you guys just get here?"

Susan beamed. "I drove."

"Wow, you got your license? Congratula—"

Before April could finish the word, Melissa interrupted. "Not just a license. Susan got a new car, April."

"Oh, wow."

"A white Camaro," added Susan.

"You go to Langley now, right, April?" Terri asked. April nodded.

"Did you get on the Pep Squad there?"

"Well, I wanted to try out, but—"

"Hey, Sue!" Robb Cochrane strode up to them. "Didja bring the car?"

Susan nodded. "My dad finally had the T-top installed yesterday."

"It is *so* cool." Melissa sighed.

"Let's see it." Robb grabbed Susan's elbow.

The girls followed them out, giggling.

April watched them go. She could have gone with them. Susan and the others had been friendly; it wasn't as if they snubbed her or anything. No one had. Her friends at Covington were the same as always—nice. Nice clothes, nice Covington homes. They hadn't changed at all. The problem was, *she* had.

Chapter 6

"You're kind of quiet, aren't you?" Toby asked in the dark of the car on the way back to her house.

"Am I?" April turned away from the lamp-lit streets to look at her friend.

"Yes, I mean, you've hardly said a word since we left Andrea's."

"Sorry. I guess I'm just tired or something."

"Party hearty, huh? Are you glad you came?"

"Sure," April answered. "Thanks again for, you know, inviting me and everything. And for the ride."

"Oh, April. Don't be dumb. Of course I'm going to invite you and everything. And I like to drive a lot so that my parents will stop yelling at each other long enough to notice how badly I need my own car. Did you see Susan's?"

April shook her head. "I heard about it."

"It's really *fine*. She wanted a convertible but her father wouldn't get her one, so she made him put in a T-top." Toby switched the radio channel to a popular new song. She started snapping her fingers and crooning along with it. "Hey, April, do you think I look okay tonight?"

"Yeah, you look cute. I like your haircut."

"But I mean my skirt. Is it too short? I mean, am I too . . . big to wear it this short?"

"No, Toby. You look good. Really. You are not too big."

"My mother calls me fat. I hate that word. I liked it better when she used to say 'chubby.' That sounds cuter. And I weigh the same as when she called me chubby, so I don't know what the difference is." Toby sighed. "Anyway, we had an argument about this skirt. She said it was too short for me, and I said I was compromising anyway because I wanted a suede one instead of leather. Don't you think suede is better than leather? I mean, everybody has leather now. Suede is more . . . you know . . . like, chic or whatever."

April tried to perk up and get involved in the conversation. What would be better, leather or suede? A month ago it would have mattered. Suede or leather. It would have made a difference.

"At least," Toby went on, "she's not trying to tell me what I should have for my birthday."

"What do you want for your birthday?" asked April.

"Truth is, I can't decide. Either a VCR for my room or a camera. Mother and Dad are always fighting over the VCR in the living room. You know, who's going to tape what, who's going to watch what. Forget about *me* ever trying to tape anything. But if I got a camera instead, I could join the photography club at school."

Go back, April told herself. *Be who you used to be.* She tried to laugh when Toby joked about a cute boy in the photography club. She managed a chuckle. Toby was making an effort, April knew. She was trying to keep up their friendship and stay close. The least April could do was hold up her own end.

But somehow she felt as if she wasn't even in the same car with Toby. Instead she was out on the sidewalk watching her friend drive by.

Toby lived in a different world now. She hadn't said a word about April's apartment, or about crowded, grubby Wilcox Avenue. Apparently, it was too different and too awful for Toby even to mention it.

April ached to talk, not about cars and leather skirts

53

and VCRs, but about what was happening to her. But she couldn't talk to Toby or to anyone else at Andrea's party. They lived in a clean, safe world, enclosed under a big glass bubble. Not Toby, Lauren, Wilsey, or any of the others knew what was on the other side. They had no idea how easily that bubble could break.

"Ms. Morgan, allow me to introduce you."

April followed Mr. Wortham's wave to the front of the Speech and Drama League meeting Tuesday afternoon.

"People, this is April Morgan, a new member of the S.D.L. She's also new to Langley, a sophomore, and I believe she'll add a lot to our efforts this year. I'm assigning her to team up with Maribeth Clayton and Lisa Hoenig for today's exercises. Would you make yourselves obvious so April can join you?"

Two girls raised their hands. April smiled. They sat with the Glamour Girls.

"Hi," April said as she slid into a chair near them.

The girls both smiled, answered, "Hi," then went back to talking with their friends.

April looked over the handout Mr. Wortham had given everyone.

"Now remember," he said, "this is a group exercise. In fact, its success depends more on the cohesion of the group than on the stellar brilliance of individuals, all right?"

Maribeth turned around.

April smiled again. "I'm pretty new to all this."

"Oh, it's not hard." Maribeth poked Lisa, who eventually stopped talking to the other girls. 'Let's get to work, Lisa."

After a few minutes the three of them had come up with an impromptu skit based on the topic Mr. Wortham had assigned them—relationships between mothers and daughters. April felt nervous every time she spoke up with an idea. Lisa and Maribeth were both juniors, and had been in the League a long time. They acted almost bored with the exercise.

April grew ten times more nervous when groups began presenting their skits.

First went a boy and two girls with a serious skit about the city's new antismoking ordinances. Then Mason Doherty and a couple of other guys walked to the front of the room. At least, April *thought* it was Mason. He looked so different that for a second she wasn't completely sure.

He seemed about a foot taller and twenty pounds heavier than the last time she'd seen him. Gone was his easygoing, happy look. Now a stern frown rumpled his face. With feet planted wide apart and arms held tensely at his sides, he boomed, "This town ain't big enough for both of us, cowboy!"

The whole room broke into laughter.

Mason went on playing the role of the Old West town marshal, staging a shoot-out with his partners.

Next, Mr. Wortham called April's group up.

As she passed Mason's desk, she saw him wink at her.

"You show 'em, little filly," he whispered.

That made her smile. It also made the queasy butterfly feeling in her stomach relax just a little.

But as she reached the front of the room with Lisa and Maribeth, the butterflies fluttered in again. All those faces staring back at her. For a moment she froze, glad that Maribeth's and Lisa's lines came first.

"Mommy, I want a cookie," Maribeth whined in a little-girl voice.

"Forget it. You've had three cookies already today," Lisa answered.

April took a breath, praying that she could deliver her lines as the little girl's grandmother without sounding as shaky as she felt. In the back of her mind she remembered Andrea Nelson's advice at the cheerleader tryouts: *When you're nervous, smile. Smile big. Look right back at people.*

It happened automatically. The joy April had felt when she made Pep Squad came rushing back to her, giving her a sudden shot of confidence. She knew her pretty smile and good looks were assets. More important, though, she remembered what Mr. Green had said: *You're no giver-upper. I'm going to hear you making a splash.*

"Now, now," she began, "why not indulge the poor child. Another cookie does no harm."

She stumbled over part of the line, and her voice was a little shaky, but underneath it was a brightness that even she could hear.

At the end of the skit, Lisa, playing the mom, hid under a table and ate all the cookies herself. The audience laughed and clapped. Mason shot April the thumbs-up sign.

Mr. Wortham nodded. "Good job. All three of you are good on the projection."

Although she wasn't quite making a splash yet, April felt glad that at least she had taken the plunge.

The next day at lunch, April headed for her bench outside. Every day she sat alone, eating in a hurry, afterward heading for the library.

Today, halfway to her bench, she slowed her pace. How much longer would she sit by herself? She had been expecting things to be the way they were at Covington, where she knew everybody and never sat alone for long. People always came over to talk to her. Rarely did she have to go out of her way to find company. Those habits were hard to break. But she'd definitely have to break them if she wanted friends at Langley.

In the cafeteria she spotted Yoko at a table with her friends. April had seen them around before. The

"Weirds" was how she thought of them. Arty types. They wore the most bizarre clothes she had ever seen—odds and ends from thrift shops, it seemed, and totally unpredictable hairstyles.

Standing in the cafeteria doorway, she half-considered saying hello to Yoko. At least they had already met. Quickly, she changed her mind. She wasn't in the mood to be snapped at again.

The sound of high, bright laughter broke into her thoughts. April swiveled to see Maribeth, Lisa, and some of the other Glamour Girls sitting at a table nearby.

She made up her mind and strode toward them.

"Hi," she said.

Lisa turned. "Oh. Hi."

Maribeth smiled. "Hi, April."

"Thanks for helping me with the skit yesterday," April said. "I was so nervous."

"No problem." Lisa smiled again.

One of their friends said something about a party the week before and Lisa laughed.

April waited. Surely they'd turn back around. They'd invite her to sit with them. At least they'd talk to her.

But they didn't. One of the other girls leaned forward to tell Lisa more about the party, and Maribeth leaned toward her to listen. They turned completely away from April.

April's cheeks stung. Should she wait, just stand there like an idiot while the Gee Gees ignored her? Maybe that was how you made friends at Langley, by letting people like the Glamour Girls snub you, or people like Yoko snap at you, or by letting the skinheads insult you.

April wasn't going to wait.

Still burning with humiliation, she walked back to her bench on the patio.

In the library after lunch, she forced herself to concentrate on her trig homework rather than think about how crummy life had been lately. It was slow progress.

She had only gotten to the third problem when she heard someone drop a stack of books on the table.

"Hi."

April looked up. A tall, slim boy with brown hair smiled down at her.

"Mason! Hi!"

"Are you trying to study?"

" 'Trying to' is a good choice of words. Not succeeding much." April shook her head.

"Sorry. Didn't mean to interrupt."

"No, you didn't. I mean, I wasn't getting much done anyway."

"In that case, can I sit here?" Mason asked.

April smiled. "Sure."

He folded his long arms and legs into the chair, reminding April of a life-size Gumby doll. Flexible and elastic, his face and body seemed to be able to change from moment to moment.

"I really liked your skit," April said. "You were such a perfect marshal."

"Oh, yeah?" Mason puffed his cheek out, pretending to chew tobacco. "Well, little filly, there ain't too much to it."

April laughed. "How do you do that? For a second you looked just like that character again."

Mason grinned. "I *sounded* like him. It's your imagination that fills in the looks."

"Okay, but you could have fooled me. Is that what you do in the tournaments?"

"Sometimes," Mason replied. "Impressions are kind of my specialty. I try to fit them into the impromptu category. By the way, which area are you interested in?"

April shrugged. "I have no idea. I'm just trying to learn about it all right now."

"Did Wortham give you the category list?"

April nodded. "Debate, oratory, one-act plays, duets, impromptu . . . I guess I'm leaning toward oratory for

58

a specialty. Prose and poetry reading. Is that really geeky?''

Mason shook his head. "Nope. It's one of the toughest categories, is what it is. Hey, Wortham isn't going to stick you with the Gee Gees again, is he?''

Before April could stop herself, she muttered, "I hope not.''

Mason laughed. "They can be pretty cold. Snobby even, I'd say. I mean, they do okay in the League, getting along with people when they have to. But they sure aren't the most friendly types around.''

"You can say that again. While we're on the subject, can I ask you a question?''

"Shoot, little lady,'' Mason drawled marshal-style, aiming his thumb and forefinger at her like a pistol.

"Well, this may sound weird, but . . .'' She took a breath. "How do you make friends around here?''

"At Langley?'' Mason raised his eyebrows.

April nodded. "I've been striking out.''

He spread his palms open. "Hey, what do you call *this?*''

Puzzled, April frowned. Then she opened her mouth and shut it, totally flustered. "You mean—''

"Yeah, *this.* Aren't you and I friends?''

A blush rose to April's face. She looked down, then back up. "Yes, I guess we are.''

"Sure we are.'' Mason nodded, then slipped into his Western drawl. "You want more friends, little lady? Why, I reckon I can round up a whole posse of 'em for ya.''

April laughed. "I'd settle for one or two. But everyone at Langley seems so . . .''

"Odd?'' Mason supplied.

"Well, some people do.''

"Like the Artsies, right?''

"The who?''

"Oh, you know.'' Mason rolled his eyes. "They wear

59

feathered hats and stuff. Make it a point to be different.''

"Oh." April lowered her voice. "I've been calling them the Weirds.''

"Hey, that fits better. I like it. Weirds. And you already know about the Glamour Girls, right? Real princessy, dress to the nines, join all the clubs. Live in Vickers Oaks, most of 'em. So do I, though, so I guess I shouldn't be talking." Mason took off his glasses and cleaned them with his shirttail. "Then there are the other groups. The jocks, of course. Every school's got 'em. And the druggies. They just float around most of the time.''

April shook her head. "It's strange. Some people did drugs at Covington, but not so . . . obviously.''

"Langley's a lot bigger than Covington, remember? A lot more kinds of people here. But don't let any of this get to you, kid. Some groups are shut tight, like the Gee Gees, but mostly things are pretty open. There are so many different crowds that you're going to find friends somewhere, I promise.''

"How about you?" April asked. "What's your crowd?''

He shrugged. "Oh, I'd probably be slotted into the 'Holier Than Thou' category.''

April smiled. "The what?''

"Oh, you know. Make good grades, don't cause trouble. Overall nerd.''

"You don't seem nerdy to me.''

Mason reached over and patted her on the back. "That's what friends are for. Pad my ego. More, more.''

April kept smiling. She and Mason *were* friends. She really enjoyed being with him. But she had never been friends with a boy before, at least not since grade school. After that she had only dated boys or small-talked with them—never been real friends.

She glanced around the library. At Covington, if a

60

girl sat alone with a boy or talked for more than a couple of minutes, people would start to stare. Later they'd ask about it. *Are you going out? Do you like him?*

Here, nobody paid attention to her and Mason sitting together. It seemed to feel perfectly normal to him, too. He wasn't flirting or teasing. No big deal.

"I've got to get to biology," Mason said. "What's your next class?"

"English. Upstairs."

"So's mine. Let's go."

They scooped up their books and headed out, chatting about the S.D.L. For the first time at Langley, April didn't have to walk to class alone. The halls felt warmer now, not so loud and hollow. When Mason turned into his class, April waved good-bye. He bowed low, like one of the Three Musketeers.

April hummed. Having friends—even just one—made a big difference.

In a few minutes, as she neared her class at the end of the hall, she spotted a group of guys leaning against the far wall. She saw their white T-shirts and cuffed jeans.

Her breath caught. The skinheads. Dragon tattoos. Big black army boots. Over the weekend there had been an article in the paper about a skinhead rally in a town not far to the north, where they shouted slogans like "White Power."

For April to get to her class she would have to walk straight toward them. She kept her eyes on the linoleum floor. There were dozens of people all around. The skinheads couldn't possibly notice *her,* she thought.

"Hey, little girl."

April kept walking.

"Sweet stuff! Come here!"

Just another few steps and she would be in her classroom.

61

"Hey!" A hand closed around April's arm. "Don't you hear us talking to you?"

April looked up to find she was surrounded. The hand belonged to a short, heavy boy. He released her arm, but now she felt even more trapped. Five boys circled around her, closing her in.

April's pulse thudded in her throat. She felt ill and furious at the same time. Who did these jerks think they were? She wanted to kick and punch her way past them, but they stood together like a solid wall.

"What do you want?" she murmured.

A couple of the boys laughed.

Another one whispered, "What do you *think* we want, little girl?"

A wave of nausea swept through April, along with deepening anger, and something new—fear.

Suddenly another hand was on her arm, pulling hard. And there were shouts. Someone cursed.

April felt herself propelled through the wall of skinheads out into the open. The hand stayed closed around her wrist, more like a bird's talons than anything human.

"Pick on someone your own size!" a high voice screeched. "Like a *worm!*"

April focused on the small figure beside her. At first all she saw was a mouth outlined in dark purple. It shouted curses at the skinheads. The she saw the black sheaf of hair, and a big necklace of colored beads painted with the letters Y-O-K-O.

"Come on!" The hand jerked at her again, pulling her down the hall. "What's your problem?" the purple mouth asked once they were safe inside the girls' rest room.

Still catching her breath, April gasped out, *"My* problem?"

"Yeah, you. Who do you *think* I'm talking to?" Yoko turned away and pulled a comb from her back pants pocket. She fluffed her hair with it, then shook her head.

"How stupid can you get, letting those clowns corner you? Wake up, for chrissake!"

"It's not *my* fault they surrounded me. I was just—"

"You were just looking like you usually do. Stupid. All doe-eyed and pie-in-the-sky. No wonder they hassle you, Miss Teenie America. You're walking bait."

April narrowed her eyes. "Look, Yoko. Thanks for the help, but I don't have to listen to *you* hassle me, too."

Yoko grinned. It was more like a crack in her small face than a smile. She put her palms together and clapped. "There you go! Congratulations. See? When you're teed off, show it! Don't be a victim."

"Thanks." April bit the word out. "I'll remember that. I'm late for class now. Good-bye." She flung open the door and stormed out.

The sound of Yoko's laughter followed her down the hall.

Chapter 7

April hardly heard a word of Ms. Herrera's talk in English class. She was still trying to sort out what had happened. Yoko Rodriguez had helped her escape a gang of skinheads.

No. Yoko hadn't just helped her. She had downright *rescued* April, when no one else in the hall had even bothered to say anything.

When someone rescues you, you don't act rude to her, do you? Even if she's rude to you first.

63

April bit her lip. It was funny, how her behavior toward Yoko was the main thing on her mind, instead of the ugly scene with the skinheads. Somehow, she felt much less fear of them now. Mostly she was furious. Later, maybe she'd report them to the principal. For the time being, she owed Yoko Rodriguez an apology—a big one.

At the lockers after last period, a small, dark-haired head faced away from April. Yoko grabbed an armful of books and stuffed them into a huge canvas bag with a peace symbol patch stitched on it. April could hear her smacking her gum.

"Excuse me. Yoko?"

The girl turned. More gum-smacking. "Yeah. Oh, it's you."

"Yes, it's me. I, um, I just wanted to say I'm sorry if I was rude after—you know. Earlier today."

"*If?*" Yoko let out her snort of a laugh. "You were rude, all right." She dropped one more book into her bag and banged her locker door shut. "You know what?" Her jet-black eyes squinted up sideways at April.

"What?"

"I've got shocking news." She took a step toward April and whispered. "So was I."

April half smiled. "You? Rude? *Nah.*"

Yoko let out a belly laugh. Then she looked April right in the eyes. "I knew I'd find a reason to like you. Gotta go now to catch my ride. See you tomorrow, okay?"

"Okay," said April, and waved.

The next morning she was hanging her jacket in her locker when she felt a hand grip her arm. She whirled, a book in one hand, ready to throw it.

"Hey, it's me!" Yoko laughed. "Just testing you."

"Oh, great." April patted her chest in relief. "Give me a heart attack."

"Yeah, but you didn't *look* scared. You looked mean. That's good. You're learning." Yoko opened her locker. "Where'd you come from, anyway?"

"You mean before Langley? Covington. We had to move."

"Right, Covington. I should have known."

"What's that supposed to mean?" April raised an eyebrow.

"Hey now, don't get huffy, Miss Cov. I just meant you probably didn't have . . . you know, skinheads and stuff there."

"We did, actually. Just not as many of them, I guess. And they weren't so bold about it."

"Yeah. Ours can be pretty bold. I don't think they're going to hassle you anymore, by the way. In case you were wondering. If you either totally ignore them, or stand up tough enough to them, they back off."

"I've been wondering whether or not to report them to the principal," April confessed. "I mean, is this the kind of thing they do? Do they bother other people?"

"They're jerks." Yoko rubbed her small, upturned nose with the back of her hand. "Everybody knows about them. The principal, too. Usually they try to pick fights with black or Hispanic kids. But people are pretty cool about it. We ignore them. Just don't act like a victim, you know. Like I said."

April nodded.

"Which way's your homeroom?" Yoko asked.

The two girls started walking together.

"So." Yoko pushed a handful of brass bangle bracelets up her forearm. Each of her fingers wore a ring— some silver, some brass, and some plastic ones that looked like they had come from gum machines. "Where do you live now?"

"Easton," April answered.

"Hey, that's where I live. Rutland Avenue. Know where that is?"

65

April shook her head. "We just moved to Easton a month ago. To Wilcox Avenue.

"Wilcox? Wow. We're practically neighbors. I'm two streets away."

"Really? Why don't I ever see you on the bus?"

"Oh, our next-door neighbor drives me on her way back and forth to work. I live with my grandma."

April nodded. "Well, here's my homeroom. See you at lunch? You can fill me in on the neighborhood, okay?"

Yoko tossed her head back with a laugh. "Hah. That would take longer than lunch. See ya, Cov."

BeeBee Wilson wore an orange tie-dyed turban, matching scarf, and green argyle knee socks. Chandra Jenkins had painted her eyelids with red glitter. Every square inch of her jeans bore a sewn-on patch: different countries' flags, Boy Scout emblems, an image of Earth with the caption *Home*. They were Yoko's friends, but to April they seemed almost like characters from a science-fiction movie.

Sitting beside them at lunch, she knew she must look pathetically normal in comparison. True to the Langley tradition, though, no one even glanced twice in their direction. That was just how it worked at Langley. You could be a giant green tarantula in the middle of the cafeteria, and you might provoke a yawn or two. Live and let live.

A very, very different attitude from Covington's.

By the end of lunch period April found herself having more fun than she'd had in weeks. Chandra could sing and did so often during the conversation—anything from pop tunes to gospel songs she knew from her church choir. BeeBee was pretty quiet, but Yoko got her to tell April about her poetry, which had been published in a teen magazine. She promised to let April read it and

66

maybe even use a poem in a speech tournament some-time.

On the bus home after school April smiled to herself, imagining what Lauren or Wilsey would think of her new friends. One look and their eyes would pop right out of their heads!

Unlocking the apartment door, April heard the phone ringing. She dashed in, fastened the locks behind her, and ran to answer it.

"Hello?" she panted.

"April, hello! It's me."

"Dad? Hi! How are you?"

"I'm fine, angel. How about you?"

"Oh . . ." April flung off her book bag and collapsed onto the sofa. "I'm fine. Things are going okay at school. I'm getting, you know, involved and everything. But I guess you don't know about all this because it's been so long since—"

"That's great, April," Dad interrupted. "So you like the new school?"

"It's all right."

"How's Sean? Is he home yet?"

"No, he's got soccer practice three days a week. Didn't you know he joined the team here? Gosh, it's been weeks since we talked to you."

"Yes, it has, honey. I'm sorry. I tried to call, but I couldn't reach you."

"Oh, we weren't home?"

"You *moved.*"

"Well, yeah. That was a long time ago."

"I didn't know about it until last week."

April paused. "You didn't know?"

"Your mother sent me a note. It arrived yesterday. Until then all I knew was that the phone had been dis-connected."

"Wait. Mom didn't tell you before?"

67

Silence from Dad. He seemed to realize he had entered deep water.

Finally he said, "No big deal, honey. Just a miscommunication. Now tell me something. When are you coming to see us?"

They talked about the Thanksgiving holiday next month and the guest room Dad had prepared for her and Sean. But April still felt shocked. Why hadn't her mother told Dad that they were losing the house in Covington? That meant that Mom hadn't even *tried* to get money from Dad to help make the payments. Dad should have been the first person for Mom to turn to. Keeping a roof over April's and Sean's heads was their father's responsibility as much as their mother's.

For that matter, why hadn't Dad been making his support payments? April had tried not to think about it. She didn't want to blame losing the house on Dad alone. Like Mom said, he had new responsibilities nowadays. But what about his old ones?

A spark of anger toward her father flickered in April's heart. She doused it quickly. The last thing she wanted was to be mad at Dad. She loved him. She loved Mom, too. Yet she couldn't help thinking about the fact that none of this—losing the house, leaving Covington High, moving to Easton—would have happened if either Mom or Dad had done things differently.

She didn't understand them at all.

"Hey, April! Want a ride home?" Yoko yelled across the broad yard in front of the school building Tuesday afternoon.

April peered above the crowd. She spotted Yoko next to a bright-yellow Volkswagen, waving her arms as if she were directing airport traffic. April made her way to the sidewalk.

"I already asked Mazie," Yoko announced. "Mazie Summers, this is April."

A middle-aged black woman leaned across the seat and smiled. "How do you do, April? I hear you're a neighbor of ours."

"Are you sure it's not out of your way?" April was delighted by the idea of not having to ride the bus, but she remembered that back in Covington, car-pool parents never varied from their routes. An extra block was a big deal.

"Out of my way? Heavens, to Wilcox Avenue? Come on in."

Yoko climbed into the backseat and let April have the front.

On the way, Mazie kept up a steady conversation about her twenty-year job as a buyer at one of the big department stores downtown. Yoko complained that the bags of groceries in the backseat were falling over into her lap.

That evening at dinner, Mom balked at first about April riding with "strangers," but finally agreed to let her accept Mazie's offer of daily rides.

"I suppose it's more pleasant than the public bus, isn't it?" Mom murmured as she cleared off the dinner dishes. "And it's very kind of this . . . Mazie. Would you ask your friend for Mazie's phone number so I can thank her?"

April nodded and called Yoko. Mom then phoned Mazie to make her thank-you's, and also, April suspected, to run a telephone personality check and assure herself that sweet old Mazie wasn't some sort of psycho.

Mazie passed with flying colors. April wasn't so sure, though, of what Mom would think of Yoko.

For instance, the next day at school Yoko wore a red felt hat with a red mesh net veil over her face. She had on red plaid leggings topped by a droopy, oversized red sweater, and white high-top sneakers.

"Where did you get *that?*" April asked, pointing at the hat.

69

"Like it?" Yoko grinned. "My grandma's. Can you believe she used to wear stuff like this? It's so sexy. You wouldn't believe it, if you knew my grandmother."

April fingered the delicate veil. "Pretty." She found herself wishing she had the courage to dress like Yoko and some of the other Weirds, or Artsies, as some of them called themselves. It might be fun—wearing absolutely anything you felt like wearing. Army surplus one day, a "Mod" sixties miniskirt the next, or a fake feather boa. Costume of the day. April's own jeans and skirts were boring in comparison.

"Hey, why don't you come over and meet Meemaw?" Yoko suggested. "My grandma. She's from Japan. She'd like you. You're so straight. She probably thinks there aren't girls like you around anymore."

April narrowed her eyes at Yoko, half grinning. "I'm not sure how I should take that."

"A compliment, definitely. Meemaw's gonna love you."

The next afternoon Meemaw made tea for the girls. They sat in the parlor of her old Victorian row house on Rutland Avenue. That was what Yoko had called it—the parlor—as she ushered April in, and that was exactly how it felt to April. She perched on the edge of a green velvet love seat, sipping from a rose-patterned cup. There were tassel-fringed lamps and crocheted doilies. Yoko's tiny grandmother sat in a rattan chair next to April, looking exactly like someone who belonged in a parlor. She wore a gray dress with a white lace collar, pearl earrings, and nothing but smiles on her fine features. With clear, dark eyes and few wrinkles, she seemed more like a fading flower than an old woman.

"Should I get more hot water for tea, Meemaw?" Yoko asked quietly.

Her grandmother nodded in her slow, graceful way and said something in Japanese. Yoko had explained that

70

Meemaw understood English, but didn't speak it very well.

"She says to tell you she's very pleased you've come," Yoko translated.

Meemaw nodded again, smiling at April.

Standing behind her grandmother, Yoko winked and mouthed at April, "Told you so!" She bent over and enveloped Meemaw in a soft hug.

April could hardly believe what she was seeing. How could the gentle girl kissing her grandmother's hair be the same as the prickly, gum-snapping Yoko from school?

"How d'ya like Meemaw?" Yoko asked as they walked upstairs to her room after tea.

"She's beautiful. And sweet."

Yoko laughed softly. "She puts up a good front. My Meemaw. A Marine drill sergeant in disguise. But we're a team."

"Have you always lived with her?"

Yoko shook her head. "I was an army brat for a long time. My father's a colonel. Want to see his picture?"

Yoko opened the door to her room.

"My gosh!" April gasped.

Yoko's room was a burst of color. Painted sheets in shades of russet and aqua draped the walls and ceiling.

"This is wild," said April.

"Thanks. I take that as a compliment. I made the hangings. Didn't know what else to do with them."

"Really? You made them?"

"Yeah. It's silk-screening. I do it in art class at school."

"Yoko, these are gorgeous."

"Aw, come on. They're not *that* great."

"But *I* can't do anything like this. I'm not artistic at all." April fingered the soft fabric shot with swirling patterns. "Really gorgeous."

71

Yoko crossed her arms. "You don't have to lay it on so thick."

"What?"

Yoko shrugged. "I don't know. I didn't invite you over to show off my incredible artistic talent. You don't have to be polite and act interested and stuff."

A sharp, sarcastic tone had crept into Yoko's voice, much like the one she often used at school. At the same time, though, April sensed a very different undertone. Yoko sounded shy and unsure, as if she wanted to cut herself down before anyone else got around to it. Under the tough act lay another side of Yoko.

April shook her head, smiling. "Considering the fact that *I'm* all thumbs when it comes to any kind of artwork, it's true that I'm going to be impressed by just about anything you show me. But I'll try not to compliment you too much, okay? I'll try really hard to be rude, too. Happy now?"

Yoko made a face at April. "You're too much of a smart-mouth to come from Covington, you know?" She chuckled. "Well, anyway, here's my dad." She pointed at a framed photograph on her nightstand. It was of a handsome man in a uniform. Wavy black hair, a dark mustache, light-brown skin.

Next to it was another picture. A pretty Japanese woman in a flowered dress holding a toddler's hand. They were in a meadow somewhere, a puppy frolicking at the toddler's feet.

"That's me. The kid. And my mom. She's dead. And Taffy the dog."

"Oh. I'm sorry." April picked up the photo.

Yoko shrugged. "Yeah."

"How old were you?"

"Four. She had a heart condition."

"So you grew up with your dad on the army bases?"

"Yeah, it was rotten. Our life was really . . . unstable. A lot of the kids did drugs. And the ones who didn't

72

were pretty stuck-up, you know. I hated it. I kept trying to tell Dad. He wouldn't listen. He stayed busy with his work and everything. And he wouldn't accept that military kids could be jerks. So I ran away."

"You *ran away?*" April repeated in horror.

Yoko nodded. "That wasn't so great, either. If you're ever tempted, come talk to me first. I don't recommend it much."

"When did that happen? Where did you go?"

"Two years ago. I was thirteen. I was *trying* to get here to my grandma's house. But it was four states away. That's a long way for a kid. When my money ran out I couldn't ride the buses anymore. I got stuck in a shelter in Chicago."

"A shelter? You mean a—"

"Homeless shelter." Yoko shuddered. "Does your nose work very well?"

"What?"

"Your nose. If you've got any kind of sense of smell, and you go into one of those places, you're sunk. Phew. A bunch of those people don't have places to bathe or anything, you know, or wash their clothes. Bad shape. I was a kid so I didn't have to hang out with them too much. Thank God! I would have thrown up!"

April was feeling sick herself. It wasn't just her stomach and the idea of what Yoko described, but something deeper. Something like fear.

Swallowing, she asked, "How long did you have to stay there?"

"Three days. My father came and got me. I cried a lot. He was really furious. I mean, he didn't talk to me practically the whole plane ride home. But eventually he got really upset that he couldn't figure out his own kid. You know, an army colonel not in control at home? So he finally said we were going to counseling. That helped. At least he got the point that I wanted a chance to just root somewhere, to stay put, you know? Now he lets me live with Meemaw during the school year, and he got posted to a base that's just a couple of hours away.''

Watching Yoko rearrange the photos on her nightstand, April's thoughts were somewhere else. That sick feeling stayed with her. In her head swirled images of old men, old women, and young mothers with small children all crowded onto a gymnasium floor. They had narrow cots for sleeping and old, thin blankets.

Where had she seen that? Television. Homeless shelters on the evening news. It was a familiar scene. But she had never thought about what Yoko said: the smell, the people who couldn't wash. If you didn't have a home, there were a lot of things you couldn't do. If you couldn't pay the rent or the bills, if you lost your home, just how easy was it to become one of those people on the news?

Chapter 8

The room was quiet. April looked up and took a breath. She held a sheet of paper with a poem BeeBee was letting her use.

"The You and the Me," she began, "by BeeBee Wilson.''

> '' *'In the light of day*
> *you come and go,*
> *a shadow, a possibility, someone*
> *who might never be.*
> *Everyone else seems to*
> *know you.*

It's only me
left in the dark.
They say no one knows
herself
before age thirty
or so.
Is that how long I have to wait and
what if I don't get that far?
Could be
I'll never see you.
Could be
today
I'll put the you and the me
together.' "

As she recited the last line, April took another deep
breath. Now it was her turn to wait. Her fellow S.D.L.
members were still dead quiet. Was that good or bad?
she wondered.

"Comments, anyone?" Mr. Wortham asked. His eyes
scanned the group, looking for someone to open the
discussion.

"Powerful piece," Sara Hawkins offered. "I liked
it."

"And the presentation?" Mr. Wortham prompted.
"Come on, let's give some feedback here. April plans
to use this selection in the next tournament. We need to
help her out."

A senior raised his hand. "Maybe too fast. You need
to slow down some."

April nodded. "A lot or a little?"

"A *lot*," the boy answered. "I thought it was read
way too fast. But your intonation was great. You really
gave it the right emphasis."

These group critique sessions were getting much
easier. Mr. Wortham had been holding a lot of them in
preparation for the tournament. During the first couple

75

of sessions, April had gone stiff with nerves, terrified by the idea of people firing criticism at her. But it didn't turn out to be so bad. It was more like a discussion. You could ask questions back, and if you listened carefully, the critiques really did improve your work.

After the session she caught up with Mason in the hall. "What did you think of my solo? You didn't say anything during the meeting."

"Nothing to add," he answered. "Just slow down, like they said. Get more practice in front of the group before the tournament to calm the old nerves. You're gonna be a contender, kid." He gave her a sideways Marlon Brando leer as they walked along the hall.

"No, seriously, Mason. Do you think I'm ready for the tournament?"

"Yes, seriously," he insisted. "You're good, okay? Pretty good, in fact. Anyway, the more experience you get in tournaments, the better."

April sighed. "I've only been doing this for a few weeks, and to get up in front of so many people . . ."

Mason shrugged. "Well, how do *you* feel about it? Do you feel ready?"

April looked at him for a moment, then nodded. "Yes, I think I am. I mean, I might make a total fool of myself, but—"

"You're not gonna make a fool of yourself, April." He slipped a reassuring arm around her and gave her a little shake. "Okay?"

His smile was friendly and confident. His arm around her felt that way, too, like a brother's. But for a second April thought she saw something else in his eyes. A searching look, like an unasked question. Or was she imagining it?

Mason let her go. "Don't worry, little lady," he drawled John Wayne–style. "You're gonna be the best or-a-tor in the West."

April laughed. As usual, Mason had made her feel

better. She left him at his classroom door and started to walk on.

"April!" he called just before she turned the corner in the hall. "Want to get together at lunch sometime? Practice our pieces?"

She turned around. "That would be great. How about tomorrow?"

"You got it." Mason nodded. "Library, twelve-thirty, tomorrow." He pointed a finger at her, shot it, and winked.

Walking backwards away from him, April was just about to turn forward again when she came to a thudding halt. Something—or someone—had run into her from behind.

She whipped her head around, heart racing, imagining the skinhead gang. But that wasn't what she found. Not at all.

"Sorry," said a deep, smooth voice.

April looked up into dark-brown eyes framed by heavy, frowning eyebrows.

A boy's hands lay on her shoulders, steadying her. He stood just a little taller than her.

"Oh, it was my fault. I mean, I wasn't—" April stammered.

"Watching where you were going?" The boy shrugged, then grinned. A very small, tight grin. "It's okay. Few people ever do." He dropped his hands. "See you later." He walked around her, and she saw his long, glossy black hair tied in a braid down his back. Over his shoulder, as if he were tossing a ball, he added, "April."

She knew she had seen him around school somewhere before. Maybe with one of Yoko's friends.

How did he know her name?

For a moment April didn't move. Watching the boy walk away, she realized her heart was still beating hard.

* * *

77

In her room that evening, April sat at her desk with her history textbook. It was eight o'clock, that quiet time of day she had always enjoyed. With dinner eaten and the dishes done, there was a lingering feeling of family togetherness, even though they were each busy with their own activities. Mom usually sat in the living room to read or work on the newspaper crossword puzzles, or sometimes talk with friends on the phone. April and Sean did their homework in their rooms.

Day-to-day life really hadn't changed much from how it had been in Covington. April sighed, feeling grateful. Things could have been far, far worse.

At least school was going okay. For one thing, she had friends now. Yoko and the other Weirds, and Mason. All afternoon, she had been thinking about that boy in the hall, too. Who was he, and how did he know who *she* was? She remembered the strong, steadying touch of his hands on her shoulders, but still she could barely picture him. A dark, serious gaze, heavy eyebrows, a long black braid. It had happened so fast. She wondered why she hadn't noticed him around school before and when she would see him again.

Get back to studying, April told herself.

Just as she started reading again, a loud blast from the television came down the hall.

Sean must have finished his homework.

Clenching her teeth, April remembered that there were some things that *had* changed from Covington. Like the thinness of the walls.

She got up and shut her bedroom door. It didn't help. The TV characters were yelling at each other. Soon they got into a roaring car chase complete with honking horns and deafening crashes.

April got up again and marched down the hall to the living room. But before she could say anything she heard her mother shout, "Sean, shut that off!"

Mom covered her ears with her hands.

78

Holding the remote-control, Sean protested, "But this is a cool show."

Mom's face twisted. It became a threatening glare aimed at her son. "I said, turn it *off.*"

He didn't wait for a second warning. Looking downright scared, he turned off the television.

April didn't blame him. Mom seemed ready to bite his head off. Sitting at her desk, she was surrounded by little piles of papers and her calculator.

Sean jumped off the sofa and ran to his room, a cloudy, hurt look on his face. April was tempted to go console him, but curiosity about Mom's mood won out.

She walked to the desk and scanned the piles of paper. South County Lighting and Power, Rex Auto Parts, First City Bank. Bills.

Mom sighed. "For heaven's sake. Would you go tell your brother to come back? I didn't mean to shout at him."

"Okay, I will. What are you doing, though?"

Mom took off her glasses and rubbed her eyes. "The usual. Juggling payments."

"What do you mean?"

"Well, the light bill is due in four days, the rent in a week, and the car payment *last* week. So for the time being the car goes to the top of the list, which automatically knocks down the other two, which means they'll be at the top of the list *next* payday."

"Will that work?" April asked.

Mom shrugged. "It has to."

April picked up one of the bills, a small, pink sheet of paper with a date stamped on it. "Mom, this insurance bill was due on the twentieth of last month. Today is the sixteenth."

Her mother nodded. "I know. It's late."

April looked over the others. "They're *all* late."

"Yes, I'm running past due on almost everything. I just—sometimes I just can't face doing this. Sitting down

79

every month and trying to squeeze these payments out of my salary. Sometimes I let it go until the next month, and then I'm that much further behind. Oh, don't listen to me, sweetheart. I'm making things sound worse than they are.''

"How bad are they?''

"It's nothing for you to worry about, all right?'' Mom patted April's arm. "Things will work out fine, sweetie. They always do.''

April bit her lip. Was losing the house part of things working out "fine"?

"Mom,'' she ventured, "you know, when Dad called the other day, he said you never told him about the bank repossessing the house until after it happened.''

"There's nothing he could have done about it.'' Mom put her glasses back on and turned to her paperwork.

"Maybe he could have sent money if he had known earlier on how bad things were,'' April suggested. "Maybe he can send something now—''

"April, sweetie, right now I have to work with what I have. I'm responsible for keeping this family afloat and I'm going to do it.'' Mom's face still looked pinched and anxious, but over that was a layer of stubborn resolve.

"I was thinking,'' April said, "about how many kids my age have part-time jobs. It might be good experience for me to get one. That might help.''

Mom put her pencil down and turned tired, red-rimmed eyes up to April.

"Mazie says,'' April went on, "that the department store where she works hires teenagers for inventory and for their stockroom.''

"Have you been discussing our finances with Mazie?'' Mom asked.

April shook her head. "No. Yoko and I were talking about summer jobs, and I was thinking maybe I could get one now, instead.''

"I'd like you to go back to your room and finish your homework, April."

"I will, but—"

"You are *not* going to get a job, do you understand? Your job is to go to school and study." Mom pushed her hair behind her ears.

"But I could help out with an extra paycheck if—"

"You are *not* going to get a job!"

April held her breath. Mom's face twisted into the same angry look she had zapped on Sean.

In a thin, tense voice, Mom said, "I am tired of you constantly riding my back, April. You act like the sky is falling. We have a perfectly decent roof over our heads and we have never gone hungry. We *won't* go hungry, either. You have to pull yourself together and stop hounding me about our financial situation, all right? Leave the worrying to me. It will make things a lot easier on both of us."

Eyes stinging, April nodded. Mom never used to speak to her that way. It made her feel like a two-year-old.

Barely controlling her anger, she snapped, "Fine. I'll go tell Sean you're in a *much* better mood now."

At bedtime her mother came to April's room to kiss her good night. They didn't talk. Mom gave her a close, gentle hug, and April hugged her back. She wanted to forget about their argument. In fact, she wished she could do exactly what Mom had told her to. Nothing would be nicer than to go back to the way things used to be, when she hardly ever thought about money, much less worried about it.

Falling asleep, April had odd, confused dreams. In one, she stood at a podium trying to talk, but couldn't even open her mouth. In another she was in a large, dark cavern with eerie sounds echoing all around her.

April sat up in bed, suddenly awake. The sounds went on, louder now. She froze, slowly realizing that the

81

sounds were real. Ranger was barking and someone was screaming—Sean!

She flew down the hall to find her mother in Sean's doorway, switching on the light. Ranger dashed around the room, sniffing excitedly.

"What is it?" April gasped out.

"A rat!" cried Sean. "It was on my bed!"

"Your *bed?*" Mom's voice was a horrified whisper.

"I was asleep and I felt something move, and at first I thought it was Ranger but it wasn't. I saw its eyes, Mom. Right there!" He pointed at the foot of his bed.

"Where'd it go?" April asked. She rubbed her face. This was no longer a dream, she knew. It definitely qualified as a nightmare.

"I think—" Sean swallowed. He wasn't the type to be squeamish, but the rat had obviously made an impression on him. "I think it went under the bed."

April's stomach churned. A rat. In their apartment. On her little brother's bed. Now it might be *under* his bed, lurking, waiting. She shuddered. Mom would know what to do.

April waited for her mother to act, but Mom just stood in the doorway beside her, fingers still on the light switch.

She looked into her mother's face. What she saw gave her another shudder. There was nothing there. Mom gazed toward her son, but seemed not to see him. Her face was blank, as if she were asleep, or as if—

April felt cold. Her hands and feet turned icy. She didn't want to look at Mom anymore. If she looked, she might go to the place where her mother was. The edge of a cliff, or that echoing cavern in her dream.

Ranger's bark drew April back. She saw him stationed beside Sean's bed, ears and tail high, growling down at the floor.

"It *is* under my bed," Sean whispered. "Ranger's trying to tell us."

Suddenly the dog lunged at the space under the bed, shoving as much of himself as he could into it, barking furiously all the while.

Something gray hurtled out the other side.

Ranger dashed around the bed and flung himself into the corner behind Sean's desk.

"It's back there!" Sean shrieked.

The dog pounced again, then drew back as if something had struck at him. Low, hissing sounds came from behind the desk. Ranger barked again and glanced at April.

She didn't think. All at once, as if acting on their own, her legs took her to the baseball bat leaning against Sean's closet door.

When Ranger made another lunge at the cornered rat, the little gray creature darted out from under the desk chair and scuttled across the room.

April swung.

The baseball bat landed with a hard, sickening thud. A screech of pain filled the room, then nothing.

April forced herself to look.

Her mother gasped. Huddled in his bed, Sean whimpered.

"Stop crying. It's dead." April spat the words out quickly. She wanted to get rid of those words, along with the revulsion that threatened to overwhelm her.

At that moment something inside her changed. Like a light switch, it turned to "off." She saw the smashed, mangled animal on the floor, heard Sean's sobs and her mother's silence. But she felt nothing.

"Call the building manager," she told her mother.

Then she left the room. All she could think of was getting out. She grabbed the apartment keys and her coat. Following close behind, Ranger questioned her with his eyes.

"Want to go outside?" she asked, and clipped on his leash.

In a few moments the chilled night air bit at her burning cheeks. Standing on the Easton Arms front stoop, April watched the motley, late-night crowd of desperate-eyed men, high-heeled women, and ragged old people wander by. For once she didn't consider the danger. Wilcox Avenue held no fear for her tonight. It wasn't just because of Ranger at her side. A roiling cloud inside her made her feel invulnerable. Heaven help anyone who dared approach her. She felt ready to explode.

The turmoil in her heart was made of unanswered questions, of bitter, bitter resentment, and of the tears she had held in check for weeks. April didn't want to cry. She had managed not to since the move. She reached down for the reassuring softness of Ranger's fur. In turn he nuzzled her palm, an old, familiar touch.

A tear escaped one eye. It trickled down her cheek, soon joined by another. In a moment, she had to sit on the step. Heaving with sobs, she hugged Ranger close for warmth.

"When the plane lands," Dad said, "you and Sean get off and wait at the gate. Don't stray, okay? I'll meet you right there."

"Okay, Dad," April answered. She held the phone on her shoulder, scribbling out the schedule information.

Thanksgiving was only days away. A whole week had passed since the "Night of the Rat," as Sean called it. Time had made it easy for him to joke, but for a couple of days afterward no one had wanted to talk about the incident—least of all April.

After an hour on the cold, dark stoop that night, she had gone back into the apartment to find her mother waiting in the living room.

"Please don't do that again," Mom said.

"Do what?"

"Leave without telling me."

April shrugged off her coat. "All right." She went to bed, but didn't sleep. From the light that stayed on in the living room, she knew that Mom didn't, either.

It would be wonderful to get away from her mother and the apartment to visit Dad. She could hardly wait.

"Is it cold up there?" she asked him on the phone. "Should we bring our snow gear?"

"You bet. We're expecting a storm tomorrow, so you guys will have plenty of the white stuff to play in. We ordered it just for you."

For the rest of the week April daydreamed about cross-country skiing and snow-sledding. It kept her from thinking about her mother's empty eyes. Even looking at Mom was too hard. For the first time in her life, April was afraid of her mother.

Part of her wanted to cry out to Mom, hold her, do anything to help. But Mom's pain was like a gaping hole. You could fall right into it if you came too close.

On Wednesday evening Dad was waiting at the airport arrival gate, exactly as he'd promised. Sean dropped his backpack and ran, leaping into his father's arms for a long, tight hug.

"Hey!" April laughed. "Save some for me!"

Dad wrapped an arm around her and kissed her forehead with a loud smack. "There's plenty to go around, angel."

"Ooh, when did you grow that mustache?" She giggled, scratching her forehead. "It tickles."

Setting Sean down, Dad smoothed the reddish-brown square of hair on his upper lip. It was a few shades lighter than the thinning hair on his head. "You disapprove? I thought it looked debonair."

"It looks like a gerbil," Sean remarked.

"That's why I miss you guys so much," Dad joked. "Your flattery is overwhelming."

Laughing, they all piled into Dad's old green pickup and buckled their safety belts. "Off we go. Lacey and

85

Charlie are waiting. They're pretty anxious to see you two.''

In the dim green dashboard light, April watched her father's profile. He looked about the same as he had during their summer visit—same square face, smallish nose, and smooth complexion, much like her own. Except now he had lost his summer tan as well as a little hair at the temples. Maybe the mustache was supposed to make up for the balding, April thought.

''Hey, the upholstery's ripped in here,'' Sean pointed out. ''When are you going to get a new car, Dad?''

Dad started the engine. ''Aw, it's holding up okay. Does a good job on the hilly terrain up here. I can't afford a new chariot right now, anyway, son. But to tell the truth I have my eye on one of those new four-by-four trucks.'' He winked.

Sean smiled back, but April turned toward the passing scenery silhouetted in the headlights' glare. The thought of her father buying a new car brought to mind too many other things. She focused on the stands of trees, dusted with sparkling white and bough-deep in snowy drifts.

''This is beautiful, Dad,'' she said, settling back for the winding ride up the mountain.

''Just wait till you see our place. This time of year it looks like something from the Enchanted Forest. We've really done a lot of work on it, too.''

He was right. April held her breath when she caught a glimpse of the steep-roofed house through the woods. The long driveway snaked through a fairy-tale scene of evergreens and snow.

''Wow!'' cried Sean. ''This is *cool*. Is that Charlie's snowman?''

''Sure is. He's dying to make one with you, too.''

Usually Sean avoided playing with his stepbrother, whom he considered both too young *and* too bratty for his attention. But the white wonderland seemed to have won him over to the idea of playing with anybody at all.

86

Charlie, bundled up in a little red snowsuit, came shooting out of the house the minute they drove up. April saw his mother in the doorway behind him. Lacey's long brown hair hung in a ribboned braid over her shoulder, and her belly was huge. For a minute April stayed in the car, staring. She had never really thought about it before—the baby. They already knew it was going to be a girl. Her half-sister. Her first sister.

"Come on in, everybody," Lacey called, waving and rubbing her arms. "I've got a fire going."

Lacey nabbed Sean as he approached and gave him a little hug. Coming up the path with her backpack, April saw her brother hug back. Another first. He had never been the biggest fan of anyone in Dad's new family.

"April!" Lacey cried, smiling. "You look terrific!"

April hugged her stepmother, feeling awkward about the big round bump between them. "So do you. What is it they say about pregnant women glowing? It's true."

Lacey gave her a soft punch on the shoulder. "Oh, right. Me, the blimp. But flattery will get you everywhere."

Dad had gone off with Sean and Charlie to stow the luggage in the guest room.

"The house looks great," said April, glancing around at the stone fireplace and the polished beam ceiling as they strolled into the living room. "You guys have really done some work."

Lacey shrugged and patted her belly. "I was pretty useful until a week or so ago. We did accomplish a lot. But your dad's on his own for most of the coming month. I'm not getting on any ladders, that's for sure."

"Is that when you're due? A month from now? Around Christmas?"

Lacey nodded, her round, pretty cheeks truly glowing with happiness. "She might be a Christmas baby. We're so soppy-sentimental, we're thinking about naming her 'Noelle.' What do you think?"

87

As always, April looked back into Lacey's brown eyes and found the warmth that had kept her from being able to dislike her stepmother. In the beginning, two years ago, she had tried her best to hate Dad's new wife, out of loyalty to Mom. But Lacey was awfully hard not to like.

"Noelle," repeated April. "I love it. You know, I've always wanted a sister."

Lacey's face fell into a funny little crumple of a smile, and her eyes got misty. "I'm glad you're here, April. You and Sean."

Dinner was one of Dad's big productions. Avocado soup, scalloped potatoes, and Sean's favorite, barbecued shrimp.

"This isn't even Thanksgiving yet," Sean observed, taking another huge forkful of Lacey's chocolate cake.

"We've started early," said Dad. "In celebration."

He didn't say what they were celebrating, but April had an idea. Dad had bustled around her and Sean all evening, showing them the house, cooking for them, telling them about the public-relations consulting business he and Lacey ran from the study. It was obvious that he was very happy to be with his children. He missed them. The message came through loud and clear.

After dinner April went to him at the sink and gave him a hard, long hug. She had missed him, too. She wished divorces never happened, and that she and Sean didn't have to live apart from Dad.

Over her father's shoulder she saw a rosy-cheeked woman with her four-year-old son in her arms. Sean sat next to them in the kitchen's deep-cushioned window seat, listening to the legend of Artemis the hunger goddess that Lacey read from a book on Greek mythology.

This was good, too, wasn't it? April wondered. This new family?

She gave her father a peck on the cheek and looked for a dish towel to help him dry the pots and pans. The towels hung next to a big, white, complicated appliance Dad had said was an espresso maker. That was a special kind of coffee. April noticed the fancy gas range and the green marble countertops. It was all brand-new. It was all expensive.

An espresso maker, at the moment, would probably rank about five-hundredth on Mom's list of needs.

April was happy. She was glad to be with Dad and Lacey. Even Charlie, so far, had been lovably well-behaved. But coming from the apartment to a house like this, she couldn't help noticing the differences.

Chapter 9

April awoke the next morning to the aroma of herbs, spices, and turkey. She wandered into the kitchen to find Dad and Lacey cooking, and Charlie on the floor. Flailing his arms and legs, he was in a tantrum about not being allowed to chop onions.

It was a good thing Sean wasn't up yet, April decided. On their last visit, he had threatened to kick Charlie out of one of his tantrums. At the moment, April was tempted to give him a good shake herself. The child sure had a healthy pair of lungs.

It amazed her that her father and Lacey let the boy carry on that way. Dad would never have let her or Sean get away with anything of the sort when they were little. As for Lacey, she was a good mom, but not much of a disciplinarian. Maybe things would change once the baby came, and Charlie realized he wasn't king of the universe after all.

"Mmm, turkey smells great," she shouted above the boy's shrieks and sobs. "What can I do to help?"

"Right now, just get yourself some breakfast." Dad smiled and pecked her cheek. "We'll draft you into service later."

Charlie's tantrum began to fizzle. April glanced at him from the corner of her eye and saw that he was studying her. A sunny smile stole onto his reddened face, although he still hiccoughed. In a moment he was at her side.

"G'morning, April."

"Good morning, Charlie. How are you doing?"

After another hiccough and a glowering glance at his mother and stepfather, he managed, "Fine. Will you play with me?"

"April's going to have her breakfast," said Lacey. "So are you."

"No, I'm not," he began, dark eyebrows knitting over bright-blue eyes. He was interrupted by Sean's arrival in the kitchen.

"Hey, something smells good." Sean rubbed his belly. "Is it it the turkey? What's for breakfast?"

Soon Charlie sat squeezed in beside his stepbrother at the bar counter, slurping from a bowl of cereal and quietly admiring the older boy's every move.

During Thanksgiving dinner that afternoon April felt truly thankful. Her father and Lacey had prepared a feast, and she had never seen anyone look as happy as the two of them together. Dad glowed as much as Lacey did, patting his wife's hand now and then and giving her lots of little hugs.

In the back of April's mind, though, there was someone else. Mom had assured April that she'd be fine over the holiday. Some friends from the office had invited her to their Thanksgiving dinner at a restaurant downtown.

It bothered April to think of her mother spending Thanksgiving in a restaurant, with people she didn't even know very well. It made her feel guilty.

All weekend, in fact, April fought little pangs of guilt: when Dad bought her and Sean high-tech goggles for their day of cross-country skiing; when they took turns careening down hill on Charlie's shiny new sled; in the evenings when they soaked in the bubbling hot tub Dad had built on the deck amid snow-laced pines.

It couldn't have been a better holiday. April enjoyed sharing the good life that Dad and Lacey had made for themselves. But why should they have so much, when Mom was struggling just to keep things going? Why couldn't Dad make his support payments on time? If he had just done that, they wouldn't have lost the house. Granted, Mom didn't seem to be the best money manager around, but she had held on to the house as long as Dad had done his share.

Saturday afternoon, when her father said he was driving to the grocery store, April asked to go with him.

The road into town hugged the mountainside, giving broad views of the forested valley and a shimmering blue lake.

"I love it up here, Dad," April said. There were a hundred other things she wanted to say instead, but didn't know where to begin.

He reached across the seat and squeezed her hand. "Me, too. I'm so glad you're here with us, angel."

She smiled. "You and Lacey are really happy, aren't you?"

"In between the usual squabbles and tantrums and what-not." Dad shrugged, grinning. "Yes, very happy."

Another mile passed before he added, "I just wish— I wish you and your brother could be with us more often. Lacey's been saying the same thing. If only we didn't live so far apart."

April looked at him—his soft hazel eyes, his handsome, strong-jawed face—her father. He was so, so happy. How could she tell him what she knew she had to?

"We've been really busy, anyway," she said. "You know, moving, fixing up the apartment—"

Dad interrupted her. "Oh, yeah, now tell me all about your new school."

"Langley?" April shrugged. "It's . . . big. Lots of different kinds of people. Not at all like Covington."

"No. Good ol' Covington. Bastion of stuffy suburbia." He sat up straight and saluted like a soldier, then laughed. "You escaped just in time."

April chuckled with him. Covington *was* stuffy. There were a lot of things about it that she didn't miss at all. But it had been home for practically her whole life. Something inside her bristled at her father for making light of the fact that she had been forced to leave.

"Dad," she said, "I know this is going to sound weird, but—"

" 'Twas brillig,' " Dad intoned, " 'and the slithy toves did gyre and gimble in the wabe.' "

April smiled and shook her head.

" 'All mimsy were the borogoves,' " Dad went on. " 'And the mome raths outgrabe.' Yup, that does sound weird, doesn't it?" He knew Lewis Carroll's "Jabberwocky" by heart, and had been reciting it to April and Sean since they were babies.

" 'Beware of Jabberwocky, my son!' " April joined in. " 'The jaws that bite, the claws that catch!' Yes, but that's not what I was going to say, Dad."

"It's not? Oh, then I bet it was 'Beware the Jubjub bird, and shun the frumious—' "

"Dad," April interrupted.

"Hmm?"

April took a breath. This was hard. Dad wasn't making it any easier by joking around. "I—I need to talk to you about something. I mean, I don't want you to feel

92

bad about it or anything, but . . .'' She bit her lip. ''It's about Mom. She isn't—she isn't doing very well.''

''Is she ill?'' Dad's tone went dead serious.

''No, nothing like that. I mean, physically she's just fine. But . . . she's under a lot of pressure right now. Losing the house—''

''Oh, *that.*'' Dad shook his head.

''What do you mean?'' April searched his face.

''She's taking that pretty hard, huh?'' Dad fixed his gaze on the road ahead.

''It *was* hard,'' April answered. ''We had to move so quickly, it—''

''Listen, angel.'' Dad squeezed her hand again. ''It was a blessing in disguise.''

April's jaw dropped open. ''Losing the house?''

''You three are well out of Covington, if you ask me. I never liked it there. A place like that is guaranteed to choke you.'' The bitterness in his voice made it sound as if Covington *had* choked him. ''Now, tell me about this speech thing you're in.''

April stared at her father. She felt as if the two of them were dancing, not talking. Every time she tried to get close to what troubled her, Dad waltzed her away from it.

''The Speech and Drama League, right?'' Dad asked.

April told him about the League. She described her pieces for the upcoming tournament. He offered to coach her the way he used to years ago.

If only things could be that easy again, April thought, the way they were when she was little. That was how Dad seemed to think of her, still, as a little girl with whom he couldn't possibly discuss anything serious.

April crossed her arms, feeling a chill despite the sunshine beaming through the windshield. Dad's bitterness when he talked about Covington—was it *only* about Covington? What was he really talking about when he took those snipes at his old life?

93

She remembered her parents' divorce—all too clearly. Lots of arguments and accusations, even a hearing in court. But it was all so long ago. Five years. Nowadays Mom and Dad talked calmly on the phone about the kids and visiting arrangements. Their anger must have simmered down by now. How long could anyone, especially sweet, loving Dad, hold a grudge?

After dinner that evening it happened again.

Sean, probably to impress Charlie, started talking about cockroaches. "You should see 'em. You don't have any up here, do you?"

Wide-eyed, Charlie shook his head.

"Sean, you don't mean you have roaches *inside* your apartment, do you?" Lacey asked, halting in the middle of a sip of hot chocolate.

April wrapped her fingers around her own steaming mug. Sitting cross-legged on a thick hooked rug beside the fire, she still couldn't seem to get warm.

"Sure they're inside. I'm naming them. You know that one who hangs out on the kitchen faucet, April? That's Roscoe."

Charlie giggled. "Roscoe the roach!"

"Then there's Rosalie. She walks around on the bathroom mirror."

"Oh, Sean, *please.*" April got the shivers. Roaches made her queasy. She'd never get used to them. And it seemed she and Mom would never be able to get rid of them, either. No matter what they did, Roscoe and Rosalie and a dozen of their pals visited the apartment every night.

"Where *is* your apartment?" was Lacey's next question.

April looked up at her. Didn't Lacey know?

"The Easton Arms," Sean answered. "125 Wilcox Avenue."

"That's *in* Easton." Lacey looked at April. Then she turned to her husband.

94

He had his back to them all, choosing a record to play on the stereo.

Lacey kept watching him until he turned around.

"Hey, you guys like this? It's the Beatles. 1968." Dad snapped his fingers to the beat.

The pretty calm of Lacey's face rippled with questions. She held a hand on her belly, eyes riveted on her husband.

Sean picked up Charlie's toy baseball bat. "Okay, here's Ralph the rat." He whacked at Charlie's favorite stuffed bunny.

"No!" Charlie screamed. "Don't hurt Boinky!"

"Bam! Bam!" Sean went on, despite the little boy's furious attack on his arm. "All *right!* Ralph's dead! Score one for April!" Laughing uproariously, Sean fell backward with a sobbing Charlie still pounding on his arm.

"Sean!" Dad's voice boomed across the room.

Sean went quiet. So did Charlie. Even April sat up straight. She recognized that tone of her father's. When his voice got that deep, you paid attention.

"What has gotten into you?" Dad demanded.

Sean shrugged. "I was just doing an instant replay. The Night of the Rat. Remember, April?"

She bit her lip. Yes, she remembered.

"What rat?" asked Charlie, choking back a sniffle. "Not Boinky! Boinky's not a rat!"

"No, not Boinky." Sean ruffled his stepbrother's hair. "Sorry. I didn't really hurt Boinky. See? He's okay. I'm talking about a *real* rat. Ralph. Ralph the rat. April smushed him."

Charlie's ever-widening eyes turned to April, as did Lacey's.

"She creamed him with my baseball bat." Sean made a face. "Mom made me throw my bat away. But it was really cool. You should have seen her. She swung low, like for a ground ball, then—"

"Sean!"

"What?" Sean looked at his father.

"That's enough. Upstairs."

"Upstairs? I was just—"

"Bedtime. For both of you."

"Bedtime?" Charlie echoed. "I don't *want* bedtime."

"Daddy's right," Lacey said, pulling herself to her feet. "Come on. Let's go upstairs, Charlie."

"Da-ad," Sean complained. "Why do *I* have to go? It's only nine o'clock."

Without looking up from the box of records he was thumbing through, Dad pointed at the stairs. "I'll come say good night when you're ready."

Sean trudged away behind Lacey and Charlie.

Draining the last of her hot chocolate, April still felt cold. Colder than ever. For a while she and her father remained alone together in the den, while Paul McCartney sang on the stereo.

He was the only one of them who seemed to have anything to say.

The plane was late. Dad called the airline to check the schedule Sunday morning, then reported that April and Sean would have an extra hour at the house before leaving for the airport.

Half of April felt deep relief. One more hour before going back to Easton and to Mom. The other half wanted more than anything to leave right away, and never come back.

Her father. Was he still her father, or had he begun to think of himself as just his children's pal? No matter what Dad said about Covington, he seemed to want April and Sean to be what they were when they lived there—sheltered and innocent. He certainly didn't want to hear about them naming roaches or killing rats. What his kids had learned and become while they lived in Easton was no business of his. He had told them so in countless ways.

At a quarter to eleven, April slung her backpack over her shoulder and gave Charlie a hug good-bye in the kitchen. Dad and Sean were already loading the bags into the truck.

"Hey, you'd better stop growing till I see you again, okay?" April warned Charlie. "I don't want you to get taller than me."

"I'm going to grow *very* tall. Taller than you!" Charlie giggled. Then his face fell. "Don't go, April! Why can't you and Sean stay with me?"

"We'll be back," she promised. "Maybe after our little sister is born, we'll come meet her, okay?"

"And to play with me!" Charlie insisted, running outside to hug his idol, Sean.

"Please do come." Lacey pulled April into a lumpy hug. "Soon. We miss you."

April's eyes stung. The half of her that loved being with Lacey, Dad, Charlie, and their little sister-to-be teetered on the edge of tears.

"Listen." Lacey took hold of April's hand. "I want you to have this."

April felt something papery in her palm. "What. . . ?" she began, then shook her head when she saw the green bill. "Lacey—"

"Hush. No arguments. It's not much, anyway. Don't make a big deal out of—"

"A hundred dollars *is* a big deal, Lacey! Why are you giving me money?"

April remembered the look on Lacey's face as she had stared at Dad the night before. It had registered disbelief, betrayal, and a touch of anger.

"Because I want to," Lacey answered.

April countered, "Because you feel guilty."

Lacey's full cheeks flushed, whether with embarrassment, hurt, or both, April wasn't sure.

97

"It's not guilt." Lacey's eyes fixed on April's. "Right now you need this. I don't."

Inside April, the storm cloud brewed. It was dark and boiling, about to burst. If she stood there just a moment longer, she knew she'd lose control. The last thing she wanted to do was cry in front of Lacey.

She turned and hurried to the car.

The apartment sparkled. When April and Sean got home that evening, they stood for a moment in the doorway, taking it in.

"Mom, what did you do, spend the whole weekend cleaning?" Sean asked, dropping his backpack on the sofa so he could look around.

With arms crossed, Mom tapped her fingers on her ribs, smiling. "I happen to *like* cleaning. During the week I'm too busy to get much done. But this was a nice, long weekend, and I had plenty of time. Yes, I know I'm weird."

April laughed. "Gosh, the carpet stains are gone. How'd you do that?"

Ranger pranced around the living room, excited to have everyone home again.

"He missed you terribly," Mom said. "He wandered between your two bedrooms like a lost puppy."

"Oh, Range, you big goof," cried Sean, wrapping his arms around the dog's neck.

"How about you? Did you miss us, Mom?" April asked.

"Miss who? *You?*" Her mother pursed her lips. "Hmm, well, let's see . . ." She cocked her head.

"Mom!" Sean protested.

Mom laughed. "All right, I confess." She hugged them both.

April hadn't imagined she'd be so glad to get home. The minute she and Sean got off the plane she noticed a big change in her mother. Mom might not be a hundred percent back to her cheerful old self, but she had definitely snapped out of her blue mood. Maybe she had needed a break from her kids as much as they had needed one from her.

Maybe, too, it had to do with the apartment. It really was home now. The Easton Arms, 125 Wilcox Avenue. April had accepted that fact. Finally, it seemed, so had Mom.

"Watch this guy," Mason whispered in April's ear. "He's really good."

A stocky boy sauntered up to the stage and nodded toward the tournament judges.

April was finding it hard to watch him or any of the other contestants who had gone before him. Her stomach was a jumble of knots. She felt so nervous she could hardly catch her breath. The day of the tournament had come all too soon.

For the past two hours, sitting with Mason, she had waited her turn. Everyone who had gone so far was good—awfully good. April caught herself wondering why on earth she had agreed to enter.

Mason elbowed her. "Watch his face."

The boy's dark eyes and mobile mouth reflected every subtle meaning in the poem he recited. It was about learning to swim—very funny, but also symbolic of how people have to change to survive. The judges didn't take their eyes off him.

The next contestant, a tall girl with a cloud of brown hair, seemed to take command of the room the moment she stepped onstage. She introduced her selection, a rap-style poem entitled "Assistance."

April felt hypnotized by the soft beat of her voice. The words came in a steady flow, about standing in line at a welfare office and feeling you belong somewhere—anywhere—else.

In a dresser drawer at home, Lacey's hundred-dollar

bill lay under a pile of socks. That was assistance, too. Maybe not the kind you wait in line for at the county office, but taking it had made April feel about the same.

She should have given the money back. She should have told Lacey she didn't need it. But the truth was, April reminded herself, she very well might need it. Not this week, or the next, but maybe at the end of the month Mom wouldn't be able to pay the rent.

When the girl finished her reading, the room exploded with applause and cheers.

"Wasn't she great?" Mason asked, still clapping.

"I'm sunk," said April. "Everyone else is so good."

"You know, this is getting old," Mason interrupted. "Stop cutting yourself down, for chrissake. Who's it helping?"

April frowned. Mason had never spoken to her so sharply. Then she shrugged. "Have I really been whining that much?"

"Sorry, but you've been driving me crazy! Relax, okay? Believe it or not, we're supposed to be having a good time." He gave her a light hug, then a pretend punch in the arm. "Aw, shucks, little lady, you gotta settle yourself down."

April laughed. She felt grateful to have Mason beside her. He was nervous, too, she could tell, which was probably why he had acted grouchy. That made her feel better. If Mason, veteran of a dozen tournaments, could get nervous, then maybe being nervous was okay.

She managed to draw a couple of deep breaths.

A few minutes before her time slot, she went into the bathroom to collect herself. Combing her hair in front of the mirror, she looked back into a pair of wide eyes. They were dark-blue and intense, focused hard.

Relax, April reminded herself. You're supposed to be having fun. But she knew it wasn't just nerves that put that look in her eyes. It was *need*—a deep, driving need to prove something.

100

No matter what happened at home, no matter how her parents acted or failed to act, April had to go on with her own life. She wanted to accomplish something, despite her family's troubles.

After zipping her comb back into her purse, she straightened her blouse, took another deep breath, and marched back out to the auditorium.

Chapter 10

"I bombed," said April. "Totally."

"True," Mason agreed, adjusting his glasses. "One of the judges was yawning. Another one was fluffing her hair."

"Thanks. You're making me feel much better." April crossed her arms and leaned back on the hard wooden bench in the hall outside the auditorium, where Mason and Sara Hawkins were trying unsuccessfully to comfort her.

"Listen," Sara said, brown eyes fixed on April, "this is why beginners compete in tournaments, right? To become non-beginners."

"I'm a beginner, all right." April groaned. "What happened in there? Why was I so awful? I mean, I knew that shoes piece backwards and forwards. I practiced and practiced." She shook her head, thinking of her performance just moments before. It wasn't that she had forgotten her material—an excerpt from a humor book by Mimi Pond about shoes. She had recited it word for word without a hitch, slowly, concentrating hard.

Still, those words had tumbled one after another from her mouth like rocks in an avalanche. They landed on the stage in a big, jumbled heap, meaning nothing.

Sara pushed her brown bangs away from her eyes. "Want to know what I think?"

April nodded.

"You tried too hard," Sara said. *"Shoes Never Lie* is humor, right? Well, it didn't come out funny. You were working too hard on your technique."

"Exactly," Mason added. "That complicated sentence in the beginning. How'd it go?"

April obliged. " 'Psychic studies have proven a solid basis for the theory that talking to shoes, like talking to plants, is good for them.' "

Smiling, Mason said, "Great line. But it's such a mouthful, and you knew you had to deliver it whole, that you got bogged down. Didn't leave room for fun."

"Next time, loosen up," Sara counseled. "Get playful. If you've got a fluff piece like this, keep it light."

April shrugged. "Okay, how about this? On the shoe-maintenance tips, for instance. 'Take them out of their boxes. How else do you expect them to hear?' "

Her friends laughed. "Perfect," they agreed.

"Well, I still have BeeBee's poem to do. Maybe I won't butcher that one. At least I'm lucky she couldn't be here today, just in case I do."

Sara shook her head. "You won't. Just remember, what the judges want is the impact of the piece. They want to be provoked. You know, emotions. A real sense of contact with you, like you're reaching out and grabbing them with your words. That's what counts, much more than perfect pronunciation or whatever."

"Hey, you've done BeeBee's poem really well in critique sessions, Morgan," Mason told her. "I know you can deliver it today."

April looked up into his blue eyes, buoyed by his encouraging smile.

"I *know* you can," he repeated.

In an hour she was onstage again. Her palms were sweating and her knees felt weak, but she took the three deep breaths Mr. Wortham had shown them in the meetings. She turned toward the judges' panel, an assortment of local actors, college professors, and retired schoolteachers.

As April began her reading she let her eyes sweep across the panel, making eye contact with each judge. Then the poet's words filled her head.

. . . *a shadow, a possibility, someone who might never be* . . .

" 'Could be I'll never see you,' " she concluded, " 'Could be today I'll put the you and the me together.' "

The sound of her voice seemed to hang forever in the silence of the big room. A few people clapped—probably Mason and Sara, she thought. Then, as she left the stage, she noticed two of the judges nodding at her, and one almost smiled.

"Actually, I had a fantastic time," April told Toby the next morning on the phone.

"Getting up in front of hundreds of people to read poetry doesn't sound like much of a good time to me," said Toby.

"It may not sound like it, but it is. Even when I was bombing out, it wasn't so bad. I mean, not as bad as I thought it would be. And everyone was so great about it. Really supportive and all. Sara and Mason were . . . well, kind of like you and Lauren and Wilsey. It sort of felt like being back in Covington again." April curled her legs under her on the living-room sofa, cradling the phone on her shoulder.

Her final success in the tournament—a solid score of seven out of ten points on BeeBee's poem—and the fun with her S.D.L. friends over pizza afterwards had helped make a change in her outlook. For one thing, it had put her in a better mood for the Christmas holidays, just two weeks away.

"I wish you *were* back in Covington again." Toby sighed. "I can't help it. I miss having you across the street. Especially when my parents are in 'grizzly' mode."

"A lot of fights lately?"

"Oh, the usual," Toby answered.

"Well, we'll have a lot of time to visit during the holidays. You can come over any time you want." April had always loved Christmastime—shopping for gifts, choosing the tree, putting up the ornaments. It was such a busy, exciting season.

"Hey, remember how we helped your mom decorate your house last year?" Toby asked. "The holly and fir wreaths? All the red and gold ribbons? It was beautiful." She paused. "Oh, I'm sorry, April."

"About what?"

"Um, well, talking about your old house and everything."

"Don't worry about it." Quickly, April changed the subject. But as they chatted about Toby's photography class, she caught herself imagining that her family would have Christmas in Covington again that year, at their old house, with a tall tree in the living room and presents piled so high underneath that they sometimes fell over.

This year's Christmas would be very different. Mom was talking about getting a small tree to fit on the lamp table by the living-room window. They wouldn't be able to afford holly and fir wreaths. April wasn't even sure there would be presents.

After talking with Toby, she went to her sock drawer and found the envelope she had hidden there. Out of it she took the crisp green bill. One hundred dollars. That could buy wonderful gifts for both Mom and Sean, with plenty to spare. Christmas sure would look brighter.

Quickly April stuffed the money back into the envelope, dropped it in the drawer, and shut it with a thud.

Assistance. The word gave her a sick feeling in her stomach. Whether it was from the government or from Lacey, the effect was the same.

April believed Lacey when she said it wasn't guilt that made her want to help. It was a sense of responsibility and caring. But Lacey shouldn't be the one to feel that way. It should have been Dad.

When April got home from school the next day, she decided to make a phone call, one she knew she should have made much earlier. For days she had wanted to thank Lacey. It was the least she could do.

When Lacey answered, April felt deep relief. She wasn't in the mood to talk to Dad.

"Hi, Lacey. How're you doing?"

"April? Hi! I'm terrific. How are you all?"

"Fine. How's Noelle?"

"Oh, she's wonderful. Kicking like a mule. April, why are you calling in the middle of the day? Is something wrong?"

"No, it's just—I wanted to talk to you while it was quiet around here. I—"

"Are you sure you're okay?"

April laughed a little. "I'm really fine, Lacey. Just nervous. I want to apologize."

"To me? For what, for heaven's sake?"

"For . . . you know. For not thanking you for the—"

"You have nothing to apologize for, and all I've got to say is, you're welcome. Listen, I have great news."

"What?"

"Noelle is being very polite. She's not coming till after Christmas. The doctor says she's running about two weeks late."

"You're happy about that?"

"Very. It's a relief. I don't think I was prepared to have Christmas and a baby at the same time. My parents

105

are coming for the holidays, and Charlie is a wild Indian with his usual Christmastime excitement.''

"Are you still naming her Noelle?"

"Yes, I think so. What do you think? Any other ideas?"

"Oh, no, I love the name. It's so pretty."

"Good. But don't let me gab at you all day, okay? I know your dad will want to talk to you. He's in the study. I'll have him call you right back."

April bit her lip. "Okay."

She hung up, stomach twisted. Never before had she felt nervous about talking to her dad. But things were different now. So confused. April was angry at her father, but at the same time she longed for him to care about her and Sean and Mom. She didn't know what to think or feel anymore.

Maybe the telephone wasn't the best way to handle it. Maybe she shouldn't answer when he called back. She could write a letter.

Dear Dad,
Remember us?

The phone rang.

April took a deep breath. "Hello?"

"Hi, angel!"

They talked about the weather. A couple of winter storms had dumped six more feet of snow on the mountains since Thanksgiving. They talked about the speech tournament and how badly Charlie wanted a puppy after hearing Sean's stories about Ranger. But Dad seemed distracted, and even awkward. He seemed to be feeling as uncomfortable as April was.

Finally, he said, "Look, angel, I want to talk to you about something. I—I'm sorry about Thanksgiving. The way I acted. To both you and Sean. I—"

"But we had a great time, Dad."

106

"Let's not play games, April. You know what I mean. I—I wasn't myself. Like that thing about the rat. I really snapped at your brother for that. I should have . . . listened. To both of you."

April was stunned. She hadn't expected this. Lacey must have given him a lecture or something.

Dad sighed. "You know that your mother and I . . . We've had our problems. That's all in the past. It's over now. But it must sometimes seem to you and Sean that the divorce is dragging on forever."

"Sort of," April said, trying to understand what Dad meant. Before, she had never felt that the divorce wasn't finished. She believed her mother and father were done with their anger. Slowly, she was beginning to realize that she was wrong. So was Dad. Only part of the divorce was over—the legal part. The emotional part wasn't over at all.

"I don't want you or Sean ever to feel that you're stuck in the middle," Dad was saying. "Okay?"

April tried to concentrate. A million things whirled through her head. The bitterness that her father felt about Covington . . . Suddenly April understood. Dad's bitterness wasn't just about Covington. It was toward Mom, too, and their failed marriage. He still hadn't really gotten over it.

Was that what the money thing was all about? Dad had said he didn't want to play games with April. But were he and Mom playing games over the support payments?

The thought shocked April, yet it seemed absolutely, utterly true. A hard knot of anger toward both her parents sat in her chest.

"We *are* in the middle," she told her father flatly.

"Yes, in a way I guess you always will be, but . . ."

A key turned in the apartment door and Sean burst in, cheeks flushed from the cold and from his daily dash up the stairs. "Hi! I'm home!"

107

"Who's that?" Dad asked. "Sean?"

"He just got home," said April.

"Can I talk to him for a minute?"

"Okay." April got ready to put the phone down. She stopped when she heard her father still talking to her.

"And angel, don't worry, okay? We're going to work things out."

April handed the phone to her brother. Sitting in the living room, she listened to him talk with Dad about sports, the NFL and the NBA.

On television once, April had seen a program about Vietnamese children whose fathers were American soldiers. Now in their teens and twenties, many of the kids had never known their dads, and wanted desperately to come to the United States and meet them. They wrote their fathers long, sad letters about how poor they were and how badly they needed help.

April had felt embarrassed for the kids. How humiliating to have to beg your own father to *be* your father.

> *Dear Dad,*
> *We live in Easton. At first I was afraid*
> *just to walk to the corner store.*
> *I'm not sure that Mom has enough money*
> *for our bills this month.*

April rubbed her arms, chasing away a shiver. She couldn't write a letter like that. Never.

Then what, she wondered, would happen if Mom couldn't pay the bills?

"What's this?" Yoko picked up the tin can April had just dropped into the shopping cart on Christmas Eve.

"Chestnuts. For the stuffing." April searched the baking-goods shelf for powdered sugar.

"Three dollars and twenty-nine cents for a puny little can of nuts? What a rip."

108

April didn't answer. She was already feeling uncertain enough about splurging on the chestnuts and real whipping cream and fresh cranberries.

"So you're gonna show me how to cook all this stuff, huh?" Yoko asked. "I've never been in on the production end of a real Christmas dinner before. Meemaw doesn't do turkey."

April laughed. "Mom definitely does turkey. Will Meemaw eat it?"

"Sure. She'll eat anything. She's really looking forward to dinner with you guys. Wearing her red silk suit. Already has it laid out."

To April's surprise, Mom had asked if she'd like to invite Yoko and her grandmother to Christmas dinner. When Mom had met Yoko at the school's holiday gift bazaar a couple of weeks before, there hadn't been anywhere near the negative reaction April had expected. A couple of comments about Yoko's hair and clothes afterward, but no explosions. Mazie had been invited to dinner, too, but already had plans with her own big family and dozen or so grandchildren.

After collecting everything on the grocery list, April and Yoko lined up behind a woman and her little girl at the checkout stand. The mother wore pants that hadn't been hemmed and a blouse that was too small, as if it had shrunk in the wash. Clinging to her legs, her daughter had wide, moist eyes and tearstained cheeks. They were buying only a few things: a pint of milk, a loaf of the discount day-old bread, a jar of peanut butter.

April looked away. She didn't want to know why the mother was buying so little food, or why, when she paid for it, she counted out her money coin by coin, as if afraid to misplace a penny.

When the clerk started on April's groceries, she couldn't help thinking about those nickels and dimes the woman with the little girl had so carefully counted out. Maybe the chestnuts and other small luxuries were a mistake. Did Sean really need the grape soda April knew he loved? She had gotten it as a special Christmas-dinner surprise for him, but . . .

The clerk rang out the total on the cash register.

April sucked in a breath. It came to more than she had expected. Not much more, but enough to make her think about putting things back.

The clerk behind the counter waited. It was the same older woman who had helped April escape the goons on the corner during her first weekend in Easton.

Biting her lip, April pulled the hundred-dollar bill out of her wallet. She had brought it along just in case, hoping the grocery money that Mom had given her would somehow be enough. Of course, it wasn't.

"A hundred bucks!" Yoko whispered. "Where'd you get that?"

"It's a long story."

"I like long stories." Yoko smiled brightly.

By now the clerk was eyeing them. April handed her the hundred dollars. She had never paid with anything larger than a twenty before. The woman took it and nodded, turning it over a couple of times before stuffing it in the drawer. She counted out April's change as matter-of-factly as ever.

"It was a Christmas present," April said as she and Yoko carried the bags out to the street. A small fib.

With her free hand, Yoko popped a stick of gum into her mouth. "Rich relatives, huh? Must be nice."

"I wish," April muttered. She braced herself for more questions.

But Yoko was quiet. She was busy blowing gum bubbles. Her hair, having grown out some at the sides, was held back by a red-and-green ribbon tied in a giant starchy bow on top of her head. It made her look like a walking Christmas present.

Two months ago April would never have believed she could be such good friends with anyone like Yoko. Now, she felt about as close to Yoko as to Toby. Every day they rode to and from school together. Along with Yoko's other friends, they sat together at lunch. Still, April couldn't bring herself to talk about her worries today. Not on Christmas Eve.

On Wilcox Avenue the wintry evening wind felt crisp and clean. It blew gently at April's hair and made Yoko's long silk-screened scarf flutter like the wings of a painted moth.

The wind had swept away the car exhaust fumes and the neighborhood's usual sooty smell. Traffic lights cast alternating red, green, and amber glows on the damp pavement, giving the street its only holiday decoration. Even the anemic little elm trees seemed almost festive, their winter-bare branches drawing poetic silhouettes against a dove-gray sky. People bustled by on the sidewalks, as frantic and excited about the holidays as anyone in Covington.

"Chestnuts!" Mom exclaimed that evening as she watched April and Yoko slice them up.

Yoko glanced at April out of the corner of her eye.

April expected the worst—complaints from her mother about all the expensive items in the grocery bags. But Mom just bent over and stole a slice from the cutting board. "Mmm. I have a few surprises myself, you know."

The three of them spent the next several hours preparing the holiday dinner. Sean came in to help with the mounting piles of pots and pans, and challenged Yoko to a soap fight. It turned into a war. Even Mom joined in, lobbing a handful of suds that landed on Ranger's tail.

April was exhausted. After she and Mom drove Yoko home, she wanted nothing more than to crawl into bed. Her feet hurt from standing in the kitchen, and she had a couple of bruises from the soap war.

111

"Popcorn!" yelled Sean when she and Mom came in. He carried a huge bowl out from the kitchen.

April shook her head. "I'm going to bed."

"Oh, come on," Mom urged, pulling April to the sofa. She unfolded the knitted throw blanket from Grandma Morgan and tucked it over the three of them. "Let's sit and decompress a while. Then you two can carry *me* to bed."

For a few minutes they lounged in contented silence munching on Sean's heavily buttered popcorn, huddling close under the blanket. Mrs. Kriss, the building manager, refused to turn the heat up higher than sixty-eight degrees.

Sean flipped on the TV news, claiming he wouldn't live if he didn't hear about his favorite quarterback's knee injury. The lights on their little Christmas tree blinked steadily on and off, filling the living room with a faint twinkly glow.

There were a half dozen presents under the tree, including some from Dad and Lacey, and April's inexpensive gifts for Mom, Sean, Yoko, Meemaw, and Mazie. The small pile was a big change from last year, but at least there was something.

Stealing a glance at her mother and brother cozied up on the sofa beside her, something occurred to April: the three of them were together. They had been kicked out of their house, fought roaches and rats, and changed an ugly, grimy set of rooms into a home. Christmas presents or no Christmas presents, in some ways her family had more this year than ever before.

On Christmas morning, it was cold. A frosty sheen covered the street and sidewalks outside. Sean huffed a breath on the windowpane and drew a snowman in it.

"Can we open presents now, Mom?" he begged.

April smiled. Still in his blue plaid pajamas, her brother looked very much like a little boy instead of the

112

cool fourth-grader he tried to be. He seemed as giddy about Christmas as Charlie.

When Mom gave the okay, April picked up a small box and handed it to him. "Open mine first. You've been shaking it so much I want to see what's left of it."

He tore off the wrapping and pulled out a jumbo-size black-and-silver coffee mug. The Los Angeles Raiders' emblem, a pirate with crossed swords, glared from its side.

"All *right!*" he yelled. "This is great, April. Where'd you find it?"

"Oh, I have my sources." The truth was, she'd spotted the hideous thing in the five-and-dime store next to the corner grocer, and knew that no one but Sean could truly appreciate it.

Next Mom opened her presents—a scarf from Sean and a pair of bead earrings April had gotten at the school gift bazaar.

Sean was showing remarkable restraint about his present from Mom. He eyed it now and then, barely able to resist. April felt anxious about hers, too. In years past, Mom had been the best Santa around, getting them exactly what they'd wished for. April didn't expect that this year. It just wasn't possible. But still . . .

"Oh, my God!" Sean shrieked when it was finally his turn. He tore a gleaming new wooden baseball bat out of its wrapping. "Cool! This is it! A Louisville Slugger! Cool, Mom. Wow! Wow! Cool!"

Mom laughed as he hugged her again and again.

"Okay, sweetheart." She turned to April. "Now yours."

For a second April just stared at the box in her lap. It was covered in gold paisley print tissue with an enormous burgundy bow, the special Christmas wrapping they used in boutiques like Briar's in Covington.

Sean poked her. "Well, open it."

"Mom," April whispered. She peeled away the layers of paper and cardboard. "This is—"

"A dress." Sean yawned.

"A *gorgeous* dress!" cried April. She jumped up and ran to the mirror in her room, holding the blue silk fabric against her chest.

Mom walked in, hands in pockets, and stood behind her. "Do you like it, sweetheart? I wanted you to have something really special, in case anything came up."

"Like it?" April shook her head. "Oh, Mom, it's *perfect!"* She turned and threw her arms around her mother.

Eyes squeezed shut, April forced a thought out of her head. No worrying today, she told herself. But the thought came anyway: a dress from Briar's, a top-of-the-line baseball bat, electricity, car payment, rent. It couldn't possibly add up right.

Chapter 11

"What did your mom say?" Yoko asked April on the phone two days before New Year's Eve. "Can you come?"

"Yes!" April cried. "I'm shocked, though. I thought she wouldn't let me go to a New Year's Eve party until I turned thirty-five or so. But she likes you. I can't imagine why, but . . ."

"Hey, I toned it down for Christmas, didn't I? You didn't like my hair? I haven't looked that tame in months."

"I'm teasing you. You looked fine. Mom thinks you're intelligent, anyway. She doesn't care if you're weird. For some reason she thinks you're a good influence on my mind."

"Smart woman," Yoko agreed. "Pretty wild how she and Meemaw hit it off, huh? Considering they couldn't talk to each other."

"Well, you translated."

"Yeah. My jaw is still worn out from it, too."

"But you're ready to party, right?" April asked.

"Full blast. Chandra and I'll pick you up at eight, okay? That's when Karin's party starts, but she hates for people to be on time."

"What should I wear?" April tapped a finger on her cheek.

There was silence on the other end of the line. April could imagine Yoko rolling her eyes. "I know what you're going to say, Yoko. 'Wear whatever you want.' But really, what do people wear to parties out here?"

" 'Out here'?" Yoko snorted. "You make it sound like another planet. You worry about clothes too much."

"*I* worry about clothes? You're the one with six jillion outfits," April countered.

"I wear what I feel like wearing. Come on, stop being Miss Covington. Wear whatever you want to."

"Is the party going to be typical Artsie crowd? No glitter or glitz for New Year's Eve?"

"Hey, I didn't say that. There'll be plenty of glitter and glitz. Want to know what I'm wearing?" Yoke described a sequined yellow vest from the Second Chance thrift shop, yellow polka-dot leggings, and Meemaw's "ruby" earrings.

But the description didn't do the actual costume a bit of justice, April realized when Yoko greeted her in the Easton Arms lobby the next evening.

"Oh, my gosh!" April cupped her hand over her

115

mouth, gaping at her friend's petite figure sheathed in neon-yellow. "Yoko, you look terrific!"

"So do you." Eyebrows raised, Yoko nodded, taking in April's new blue dress. "But that's nothing new. We *always* look gorgeous, right?"

Giggling, they hurried down the front stairs and jumped into Chandra's car.

On the way to the party, April admired Chandra's lacy black "baby doll" dress and helped Yoko tease her hair into a beehive. The three of them couldn't stop laughing about almost everything, including the looks they got from a passing carload of boys.

It occurred to April how different this New Year's Eve was from last year's, when Lauren and her family had taken her with them to the Covington Country Club formal ball. Tonight there would be no tuxedoed waiters, linen-draped tables, or swan-shaped ice sculptures, but there probably would be plenty of fun.

As they got off the elevator in Karin's condominium building they heard the party music all the way down the hall.

"The Eurythmics!" Chandra cooed, swaying her hips in a little dance. "I love that song!"

She wasted no time getting to the dance floor. They had barely said hello to Karin and BeeBee at the door when Chandra pulled them all into the little dining room. It was hung with blinking Christmas lights and silver streamers. Twenty or so other kids were jammed into the room all around them.

There were no partners, and only a few couples pairing off. April didn't even recognize some of the moves the other dancers made. People just did whatever they wanted. Typical Weird crowd.

For a while April stuck to the steps she knew, the ones everybody did at Covington parties. But then she started dipping her hips the way Chandra did, and eventually found herself just moving to the music. The tension of the last few weeks and her holiday money worries began to float off, as light and temporary as the bubbles that someone was blowing onto the dance floor. She watched a trail of the bubbles drift by almost in time with the ocean-like, watery beat of the instrumental song that had just come on the stereo.

"Uh-oh-oh. There's a place I want to go . . . oh-oh . . ." A tall boy with bleached blond hair sang to the music.

Startled out of her dreaminess, April looked at the boy. He had a half-dazed look on his face. His mouth opened wide to exaggerate every vowel sound. April frowned.

Yoko sidled up to her. "That's Jonathan Sobel. He does that sometimes."

"Is he on something?"

Yoko shook her head. "Folks here tonight aren't into drugs, Cov, okay? The boy just sings, you know? That's his thing."

"Does he have to be so loud about it?"

"Hey, how else do you get any attention around here?" Yoko chuckled and went back to dancing.

April saw Yoko's point. In a crowd sporting everything from pink mohawks to "Rock the Vote" sweatshirts, it *would* be hard to get attention. Some people in the kitchen were arguing about racism, and in the living room, along with the bubble-blower, there was somebody juggling plastic King Kong dolls. To stand out in the Weird crowd, you had to be weirder.

Maybe, in some strange way, her own qualification for the crowd was just *not* being weird. In her blue silk "Miss Covington" dress, maybe, April thought, she was the weirdest of all.

Taking a break from dancing, she followed a stream of bubbles into the living room. The bubbles wafted over heads and lamp shades. Beyond the coffee table and

117

bookshelves, she finally find their source. He was seated on the arm of the sofa.

"Hi."

His voice was deep and smooth. April had heard it before. But she could barely see his face. For a second it was masked by the darkness, illuminated only when the Christmas lights blinked back on.

"I've been waiting for you. You sure like dancing, don't you?" the boy asked. He had midnight-black hair almost as long as her own. It hung around his shoulders, glistening in the dim light.

April nodded. "You're the guy I ran into in the hall a few weeks ago, right?"

He nodded back. "That's me. You're April."

She smiled. "That's me. Who are *you?*"

"Good question." He gave her the small, tight smile she had seen before, then blew another crop of bubbles. Iridescent globes the size of tangerines floated by. "I can tell you my name."

"Well, that's a start."

"Devon," he said. "Devon Riddley. You're April Morgan."

"How'd you know?"

"I asked around. Like I said, I've been waiting for you."

April wrinkled her nose. "That sounds creepy."

"Sorry. Does it seem weird?"

April laughed. "Here? Weird? You'll have to work a lot harder than that."

He smiled again, holding the plastic bubble wand out to her. "Want to try?"

She took the wand. "How do you make the really small ones?"

Devon formed a tiny circle with his lips. "Like this." The Christmas bulbs blinked on and off, lighting his face and shadowing it.

April moved closer to see. She watched Devon's

118

cheeks stretch long and hollow out as he formed the little "O." His black eyebrows looked velvety in the soft light, no longer frowning at her the way they had that day in the hall.

He smiled. Suddenly his face relaxed. His eyes fixed on April's with what seemed for a moment like a light from inside him—so bright that she felt she couldn't look away.

"Can you do that?" he asked.

She smiled. "I can whistle."

Slowly, he cupped his hand around hers. He pulled the bubble wand to his lips and blew into it so softly that his breath whispered on April's fingers.

Everything inside her turned upside down. She swallowed, astonished by the all-over tingle on her skin. A cloud of pea-sized bubbles floated over her head. She laughed when they started to rain down and pop on her nose and shoulders.

"Go ahead," he said. "Here." He dipped the wand into his bottle of suds.

She puckered her lips.

"That's right." His voice was a low murmur in her ear. "Now just aim for the middle of the wand, like you're going to make a hole in it."

April wrapped her hand around his to pull the wand closer. She blew, and bubbles swarmed from the other end.

Devon caught a cluster of them in his palm. He brought them back to her. April touched the top of the little pile. One by one they all vanished.

Her shoulder was so close to Devon's that she felt him take a breath. She turned. His eyes were on hers, dark and serious.

"I really have been waiting for you," he said. "Not just tonight. For a while."

His voice made her shiver, but she forced herself to remain still.

119

"Why?" she whispered. "What were you waiting for?"

He shook his head, smiling. "Do you think . . . Do you think there's anyone else like you?"

April looked down at her hands. Her heart was beating so hard it felt like it might leap out of her chest. She forced it to calm down, then looked back up at Devon, grinning. "You know what? I think you're teasing me. I think you've been teasing me this whole time. You're practicing your lines."

"Lines?" Devon narrowed his eyes. "You mean, for girls?"

"Exactly." She nodded. "Want to know what I think of them?"

Devon didn't answer. His face didn't move. It was a marble sculpture—all hard angles. Thin lips, a long, strong nose, high cheekbones, and chiseled stone for a jaw.

"Your lines sounded great," said April. "They actually snowed me for a minute there. I was beginning to think you meant it."

"But now you think I'm just scamming," he finished for her.

"Scamming, teasing, flirting . . . Whatever you want to call it."

Devon smiled. The stone turned to flesh again. His shoulders slumped. He clasped his hands together and stuck them between his knees. "Do you have a guy back at your old school?"

"A boyfriend? Not lately."

"Why are you so suspicious of me?" he asked.

"Why are you so intense?" she shot back.

He shrugged. "You asked me who I was. Didn't you want to know?"

April didn't know what to say. Her head was a pinwheel.

120

"Maybe I *am* intense," Devon said. "Maybe that's me."

April nodded. "Okay."

"I'd better go." He sat up straight, then pulled to his feet.

A wave of disappointment swept over April. "It's not midnight yet," she pointed out.

"Another hour or so. The year hobbles down to the finish line." He put his hands in his pockets. "I hate watching it go."

The look on his face was a question, April thought, as if he wanted to ask her something, but wouldn't.

"See you next year," he said, and disappeared into the living room crowd. In another moment she heard Karin yell, "G'night, Devon!" Then the front door shut.

At a quarter to one A.M., the streets downtown were as crowded as at lunchtime on a business day. The difference was that the pedestrians weaving in and out between Chandra's car and the other auto traffic wore New Year's Eve sequins and party hats. The street rang with the clatter of their rattles and paper horns.

"This is a zoo." Chandra frowned, trying to navigate around a very drunk man in a tuxedo.

Yoko nodded. "Whoever came up with the word 'grown-up' for people over twenty-one made a big mistake."

"What time are you guys supposed to be home?" April asked.

"I told my grandmother between one and one-thirty," said Yoko.

"Me, too." Chandra nodded. "My dad said shoot for one o'clock."

BeeBee, who would be spending the night with Chandra, glanced at her watch.

"Do you think we'll make it?" April leaned forward in the backseat.

121

"Pretty close," said BeeBee. "Will your mom get mad about a few minutes?"

April shook her head. "No."

"Wish all these clowns would get back on the sidewalk," Yoko groused. She turned around to look at April. "Want to stop somewhere and call your mom? You look tense."

"I do?" April smiled. "It's not because of being late. It's . . . Do you guys want to hear something funny?"

Stopping at a red light, Chandra glanced at her in the rear-view mirror. "Uh-oh. I know. A guy. April's got a guy story. Who was it? Somebody kiss you at midnight?"

April shrugged. "I wish he *had* been there at midnight."

"Hey, this is getting good." Yoko perked up. "Spit it out, Cov. Come on. I confessed about John Kinsky. BeeBee had to run away from Bob Greene. And we all saw Chandra's big smooch with Armando. Hold on, let me guess. Cliff Raines. He was ogling you all night."

April grinned. "Nope. Cliff is sweet, but . . . You didn't see any of *this*. He left early, around eleven—"

BeeBee frowned. "Wait. I saw somebody leave at eleven. Remember, Yoko? Paulette and Elka were moaning and groaning about it. They can't stand it when he ignores them."

Yoko whipped around to stare at April. "Uh-oh. I don't believe it. You're not talking about *Riddley,* are you?"

April sighed and leaned back in the seat. "Devon Riddley. Such a wonderful name."

"Oh, no," Yoko muttered.

BeeBee's eyes got huge.

"Tell us you're joking," said Yoko.

"Why should I be?" April frowned.

"Haven't you heard about Devon?" Chandra half-whispered.

April laughed. "You guys make him sound like an escaped convict or something."

Yoko, BeeBee, and Chandra exchanged glances.

Then Yoko said, "Cov, *you* of all people are not the one to be swooning over Devon Riddley."

"Would you please make some sense?" April demanded. "What are you talking about?"

"First of all," said Yoko, "he's the Ice Prince."

"The what?"

BeeBee giggled. "She'll never believe us, Yoko."

"Here's what Riddley does," Yoko began. "He's a tease. He goes out with girls, just like any other guy, you know. Except that, as you probably noticed, he's about three times better-looking and about ten times more . . . sexy . . . than most guys."

So far so good, thought April. That much of Yoko's story was definitely true.

"There aren't too many girls who really want to say no to a guy like Devon," added BeeBee. "I mean, he's sweet. Pretty smart, too, I hear. He won the math award at Langley last year. He's a junior now. And he's . . ."

"Sexy," finished Yoko.

Chandra nodded. "Some of the girls who have been out with him say they just couldn't believe that . . ."

"He's the one who says no," Yoko finished again. "Every time."

April turned her gaze from one to the other of her friends.

"There are some girls who have done their absolute best," said Chandra, "like Paulette and Elka, to . . . you know . . ."

"Seduce him?" April asked in a small voice.

"Yeah, you could say that," agreed Yoko. "Great word. Seduce. Riddley is un-seduce-able."

"That's not a word," BeeBee pointed out.

"But it's true, anyway," Yoko maintained. "The Ice Prince says he's saving himself. Waiting for 'the real thing.' True love. He won't date any girl more than a couple of times.''

"He's *waiting?*" April repeated. Devon's voice, saying the same word, echoed in her mind.

"That's what he says—that he can't because he's waiting for the right one. He drives girls nuts.''

April shook her head. "You're joking, right? This is too much. How many guys 'save themselves'?"

"One, at least," BeeBee assured her. "It's part of Devon's rep at school. He's out to break hearts. Everybody knows.''

"Except me," April mumbled. "He was just snowing me, after all.''

"Hey, don't feel burned." Yoko reached back and patted her hand. "He's like that, you know. Really gets you.''

April nodded. "I know.''

"Anyway . . ." Yoko turned back to face the front. "Your mother would hate him. Want to know why the guys at school don't razz him about his rep?''

April did want to know. It would seem that no guy could live down a reputation like his.

"They're scared of him," BeeBee whispered.

"Would you two please quit talking like people in a horror movie? You're giving me the creeps." April rubbed her arms. "Why are guys scared of Devon?''

After Yoko told her, April wished she hadn't asked. None of it fit. The boy who Yoko and the others described wasn't anything like the boy she had blown bubbles with just a couple of hours ago.

Devon Riddley, Yoko said, had once tried to strangle a boy at school. He used to get into a lot of fights a couple of years ago, his first year at Langley. He was fourteen, and some guy picked on him too much. He rammed the guy against the wall so hard it almost knocked him out. Then he locked his hands around the guy's throat.

124

Those warm, gentle hands, thought April. The ones that had touched her shoulders, and wrapped around her fingers.

"We didn't see him the rest of the semester," added Chandra. "The court put him in juvenile detention for a month." She pulled the car onto Wilcox Avenue and parked in front of the Easton Arms.

"Hey, don't look so glum," Yoko said. "Happy New Year, remember?"

April gave a little laugh and pulled on locks of each of her friend's hair. "Thanks a lot. Happy New Year."

Chapter 12

April believed her friends. They wouldn't have joked around at the risk of hurting her feelings.

After school Monday, waiting for Yoko at the flag-pole, April couldn't decide whether her feelings were hurt or not. If anyone had hurt them, though, it was Devon. He had acted so serious at the party, as if he really liked her. Now it all seemed to be a joke.

Huddled in her suede jacket, she braced against the icy January wind that whipped at the flag and its chain. Other guys had tried lines on her before, she remembered. But they had sounded different. Devon was different. He truly was intense, with that light in his brown eyes like a slow flame.

She could imagine someone like him having a short fuse, being fiery and too proud, maybe getting into a fistfight or two. But actually beating someone up? That part was hard to believe.

Devon Riddley was a puzzle, like one of those plastic blocks with little colored squares you had to switch around until each side showed up the same color. Devon seemed to have that many different facets and shades. April realized she didn't want to make up her mind about him until she had seen a few more of them for herself.

When Yoko came, they walked to the curb to wait for Mazie. Brown winter leaves whirled around their feet, mixed with candy wrappers and potato chip bags. As April told her about the speech tournament coming up, one of the last things in the world she expected was for an arm to slip around her friend's waist from behind, and for that arm to belong to Devon.

"So," he said. "Bet you know all about me now." He patted Yoko on the back, squinting through the wind at April. "I bet your friends have filled you in on everything."

"Not much of a bet." Yoko snapped her chewing gum. "Of course we did."

"Of course." Devon nodded. "So now I bet she doesn't even want to talk to me." He cocked his head toward April.

Yoko shrugged. "Ask *her.*"

"Why shouldn't I want to talk to you?" April looked at Devon, then at Yoko, who was rolling her eyes.

"Aren't you going to follow your friends' advice?" He crossed his arms, hunching against the cold.

"Who said I wasn't going to?"

"Well, will you go to Corky's with me?" He nodded toward the coffee shop across the street.

"She's got a ride to catch," Yoko told him flatly. "It's not that I don't like you, Riddley. You're just too much for her, okay? Lay off."

"I like that. Honest friends. Loyal, too." Devon nodded at Yoko.

126

"I can take the late bus," April said. "Would you tell Mazie for me, Yoko?"

"That you're taking the bus? You're going to go through with this, Cov?"

"We're just going to the coffee shop." April took her turn to roll her eyes.

"Okay." Yoko sighed. "Call me later."

She waved as April walked away with Devon.

He didn't say anything until they'd reached the corner. "Yoko's all right, you know. I know what she's doing."

"Really? What is she doing?"

"Protecting you. I would, too, if I were her."

"Do I need to be protected from you? Are you that bad?"

Devon shrugged. "Everything they told you is probably true. *You* decide how bad I am."

"They never said you were bad. Someone even said you were sweet."

Devon looked at her. "Well, what do *you* think?"

"I haven't decided yet. That's why I'm here."

"Fair enough," he agreed. "I have a question. Did you believe a word *I* said on New Year's Eve?"

"People say a lot of things on New Year's Eve."

"So you didn't believe me."

April stuffed her hands into the pockets of her jeans. Maybe Devon *was* too much for her, like Yoko said.

A blast of warm kitchen air hit them as they walked into Corky's.

Devon rubbed his hands together and blew on them. "Where do you want to sit? By the door, so you can leave fast if you want out?"

April laughed. "Good idea. Except I've never even walked out of a bad movie."

They found a booth by the windows. It was small but comfortable, surrounded by the after-school noise of the shop's dozens of other teenage customers.

After they'd ordered sodas, Devon leaned back on his

side of the booth and stretched his legs along the seat. He had taken off his jacket, so that now April could see the black turtleneck that outlined his compact, muscular chest and shoulders. His long hair was braided back, and today he wore a tiny silver hoop in one ear.

"It seems," he said, "that maybe you *didn't* believe everything you heard from your friends."

April shook her head. "Wrong. I believed every word. Maybe I'd like to know the reasons why, though."

"My reasons why?" A short, low laugh came from Devon. It was the first time she'd ever heard him laugh. "You're asking the wrong person. All I can give you are the facts. Maybe a couple of excuses, too."

"You really did beat a guy up, then?" April asked.

She thought she caught a slight grimace on his face. Then he sat forward and started fiddling with a packet of sugar.

"Assault and battery." He stared at the sugar packet, turning it over and over between his fingers. "His name was Kip Roemer. He graduated last year. He got a concussion and a broken rib. The story goes that I tried to kill him. That's the only part that's not true. I wanted to kill him, but I didn't try to. Does that make a difference?"

April shrugged. "Maybe it's better than the other way around."

Devon looked at her with a narrow, tense smile. "This probably isn't the kind of thing most guys talk about on the first date, right? People they've wanted to kill?"

April shook her head.

"That was the worst thing I ever did. Do you believe that? That was as bad as I ever got."

"I believe it. It's hard to believe you even did *that.* You don't seem like the type."

He nodded. "Thanks. I don't think I am, either. Not anymore. Some people don't think a person can change. But anyone can. A little, at least. I got lucky."

128

"Yoko said you had to go to juvenile detention."

"That wasn't the lucky part." He grimaced again. "My parents filed a lawsuit that got me out after two weeks. They had to promise they'd keep me under lock and key at home for the rest of the school year, except for trips to the shrink."

"You had a psychiatrist?"

"Family therapist. My parents went, too." Devon shook his head. "Listen, if you're ready to get out of this, like I said, we sat close to the door, so . . . I mean, do you really want to hear it?"

"What I really want to hear are the reasons. Is that too personal?"

Devon shook his head. "I'd like to get it all out in the open with you, out of the way. But . . . I can't give you clear-cut reasons." He shrugged, then sighed. "Want to hear some facts? In our neighborhood, fighting other kids was how you took care of things. That's not going to make any sense to you."

"Kids fight in Covington," April said.

"Okay, then here are more facts. I was a jerk. I had a chip the size of a piano on my shoulder. I hung out with mean kids and tried to be meaner."

"Then how did you just . . . change?"

"I didn't. I didn't just change. We went through therapy for over a year. It was like having a job, or taking a class. We had to go every week, like clockwork, and we had assignments."

April nodded.

"Mostly, we got more honest with each other. My parents got more serious, too, and I got a sense of humor." He shrugged. "Believe it or not."

April smiled. "A sense of humor would have helped a lot around Kip Roemer, right?"

Devon looked embarrassed, but smiled. "Hey, you're still here. Isn't my life story worse than a bad movie?

129

How come you haven't taken your friends' advice and escaped before the closing credits?''

"I think . . ." April drummed her fingers on her cheek. "I think you enjoy your reputation."

"Oh, really?"

She nodded. "Maybe you enjoy being kind of famous. A mystery. You know, all those songs about how girls love bad, bad boys?"

Devon took a deep breath, suddenly looking very serious again. "Is that why you're here?"

April shrugged. "I like mysteries. But bad boys aren't my type."

"I'm not bad anymore."

"I thought you were going to let *me* decide."

"Have you?"

April gathered her courage. A few months ago she never would have dreamed of having a conversation like this one with any boy, much less a boy like Devon Riddley. Now she was about to take an even bigger leap. Her heart raced and her palms were sweaty. At the same time she felt stronger and braver than ever before.

"I've decided," she said finally, "that I'd like to get to know you. That I like you."

There. She'd said it. At Covington, she would rather have taped her mouth shut than say such a thing to a boy.

"You *like* me?" Devon repeated.

April nodded. He wasn't going to make her go into details, was he?

His face changed. It was no longer grim and serious, but bright—even cheerful. He was all smiles. He looked very much like Covington boys at moments when she'd said yes to their invitations to go out.

"You know . . ." Devon sighed, shaking his head. "I feel like I've just taken the S.A.T. or something."

April laughed. "Was I that rough on you?"

He turned serious again. "No. I like you, too, April. I like talking to you."

She felt a thrill course through her. BeeBee and Chandra and Yoko had been right. Devon *did* sizzle. Definitely. In part it was because of his dark good looks, but there was much, much more to him than a handsome face and muscular body. He was, as BeeBee had pointed out, sweet. Maybe it sounded corny, but April saw it was true. Listening to his calm, smooth voice, April sensed something deep in this boy with the troubled past.

The funny part was that she had never been with a boy who "flirted" the way Devon did—absolutely, dead serious.

"You know, for someone with a sense of humor, you sure can be intense," she told him.

"Is that bad?"

"Different."

"I'm not going to play around with you, April. I mean, I know I'm not like a lot of other guys."

"I've noticed." She grinned.

He grinned back. "Did anyone ever tell you *you're* not exactly run-of-the-mill, either?"

April cocked her head as she sipped on her soda straw. "What do you mean?"

"For one thing, look at you. Beautiful."

Blushing furiously, April rolled her eyes.

"No, I mean it," he said. "You *are* beautiful. Don't pretend you don't know it. And I admit that's what got my attention in the beginning. But then . . . a lot of really pretty girls are hung up on their looks. You're not. Matter of fact, speaking of serious, *you're* kind of serious, too."

"Me?" April was taken aback. Her, serious? No one would ever have accused her of that in Covington. Popular, fun, friendly—but not serious. Some people had probably even thought of her as just a pretty face—an airhead.

131

Devon could be right. Maybe she had gotten more intense about things since moving to Easton. She had definitely had to grow up some. Maybe it showed.

"Anyway, now you've heard my true confessions," Devon said. "How about yours?"

"*My* life story? It's nowhere near as interesting as yours."

"Maybe not to you. For starters, how'd you get involved in Speech?"

"How'd you know about that?"

"I went to your tournament in December. You were amazing."

"You're kidding. You were there?"

Devon nodded. "I figured it was one way to find out more about you. I would have talked to you there, but you looked busy, so . . . I waited."

He asked her more questions about the S.D.L., then about how she liked Langley, and before she knew it April was explaining what it was like to grow up in the suburbs and then have to adjust to Easton. They talked about divorce, and guys wearing earrings, and what it would be like to be famous.

The waitress had just brought their second order of sodas when April noticed the orange neon clock on the wall behind her.

"Oh, no. My bus!" She peered out the window into the dusky last light of sunset. "It's five-thirty!"

Devon glanced at his watch. "Did you miss it?"

April nodded. "Twenty minutes ago. I forgot all about it."

"I'll drive you," he offered.

"Home? Oh, I don't think—"

"You don't ride with bad boys?"

Exasperated, April sighed. "That's not it, Devon."

"See what I mean? You do enjoy your rep. I just meant it would be out of your way to take me home."

"You live in Yoko's neighborhood, right? Well, I live four blocks from her, on Chestnut."

"Really? We're all neighbors?" April had missed that feeling. In Covington, most of her friends had lived nearby.

"Come on. Come meet my heap of junk. Name's Clyde."

Across the street in the school parking lot they climbed into Devon's rusty blue station wagon. "Clyde" was a good name for the old car, which was missing patches of chrome and paint like an aging boxer missing teeth and hair.

After a few coughs and sputters, the car pulled onto the street, then backfired twice before the first stop sign.

"Having second thoughts?" Devon asked.

April laughed. "I'm adventurous. How old is Clyde?"

"1973. He was my mom's during her days as a reporter in San Francisco."

"Your mother's a reporter?"

"She was. Now she does star charts. She writes the newspaper astrology column. Ever heard of motivational counseling? That's my father's thing. You know, tapping your inner essence and getting in touch with your life source? He runs big seminars." Devon gave a rueful laugh. "They're both very New Age."

April shook her head. "Like I said, *my* life story is pale."

He laughed again, this time a full, open sound backed by his eyes and a touch of color in his cheeks. April felt his happiness warm her like a burst of sunlight through the clouds.

In most ways, the boy next to her was still very much a stranger. So far, they had spent only a few hours together. But with Devon, there was never any small talk. In an hour they had already shared histories, fears, and complaints.

When Devon parked Clyde in front of her apartment building, April turned to him. "Thanks."

"Well, sure. I'm the one who made you late," he pointed out.

"I meant, not just for the ride, but . . . This was fun."

He smiled again. As she got out, he got out, too, and came around the front of Clyde.

April heard another car door shut. Looking toward the street, she saw her mother leaving her white sedan, parked a few spaces away from Devon's.

Mom's heels clipped quickly along the pavement toward her.

"Hi, Mom." April readjusted the book-bag strap on her shoulder. "This is Devon Riddley. He's from my school."

April watched her mother's eyes take in Devon's long, braided hair and the silver earring.

"Hello," he said, smiling.

"Hello." Mom smiled back. It was a polite, brief stretch of her lips. "How do you do?"

Then she turned away. Her heels clipped toward the Easton Arms door. "April, I need you to help with dinner," she called over her shoulder.

Red heat stung April's face. She couldn't believe what her mother was doing.

Mom said in an even firmer tone, "Come up now, please."

April sucked her breath in. Her cheeks prickled with embarrassment—and anger. "Sorry, I have to go," she whispered.

"Sure." Devon's face stayed absolutely still. "See you at school?"

April nodded, and hurried away.

"She was awful." April shook her head at lunch the next day, still smarting from her mother's rudeness to Devon.

"Mothers are so picky," Chandra sympathized. "Mine is. When I went out with Luke last week she shortened my curfew to nine-thirty!"

"I don't think April's going to get even as far as a shortened curfew on this one," Yoko pointed out. "Devon isn't exactly the kind of guy your mother's used to, is he?"

"She hates him," April admitted. "You were right about that. For that matter, you hate him, too. Everybody hates him."

"Wrong," Yoko objected. "We don't hate him. We just wanted to make sure you knew what you were getting into."

"What are you going to do?" BeeBee asked. "Did you talk to your mom?"

April shook her head, remembering the night before. She had walked upstairs with her mother, helped with dinner, then had done her homework and kissed Mom good night. They didn't talk about Devon. Her mother didn't even scold her for riding home with a "stranger." Like so many of their disagreements nowadays, they had just let this one slide by.

In the Speech and Drama League meeting the next day, April managed to forget about her mother, Devon, and everything else. She had to. Mr. Wortham had assigned topics for the impromptu dramatic category based on background material he had given them in the last meeting. Her topic was gun control—the pros and cons. In five minutes, she had to come up with a three-minute presentation, then deliver it.

"Not bad, Morgan, not bad." Mason slapped her on the back afterwards as they walked out into the hall.

"Yours wasn't bad, either, Doherty." She grinned at him. "How do you always manage to come off as if you've been preparing for hours?"

"Raw talent." He made a goofy face. "Hey, a bunch of us are going to a play Friday afternoon. *Candida*, the one Wortham talked about? It's at that new theater in Vickers Oaks. They're offering free seats to students for the dress rehearsal. Afterwards they'll let us talk to the actors backstage. Want to go?''

"I'd love to," April agreed. "But . . . I have to ask my mother." She sighed. She would rather not have to talk to Mom about anything at all.

Mason handed her a little scrap of paper. "Here's my phone number. Give me a call tonight with the verdict, okay? I'll be happy to provide transportation."

"Oh, thanks, Mason." Looking up at him, she found that he was giving her his Cary Grant look—charming and debonair. It occurred to her that Mason was good-looking, in a boyish way. Funny, how she had never really noticed before. Lately he had been sitting with Sara Hawkins at lunch. Maybe they were dating. April felt glad that Mason could ask her to go out and do things like seeing the play, without the pressure of it being a "date." The two of them were friends.

Mason nodded, then saluted, clicking his heels together. "I must visit my locker before next period, miss," he said with a British accent. "We will meet again ere long."

April had to get her books for English class, too.

When she reached her locker, Devon was leaning against it.

"Well, hi!" she said.

"Hi. Glad to see you smile." He shot her a look.

April cocked her head sideways. "Why do you say it that way?"

"Yesterday," Devon said simply. "The scene with your mom. That didn't seem to leave you with much of a sense of humor."

April sighed. "Maybe that's what I need—more of a sense of humor. At least around my mother."

"She doesn't like me, huh?"

As usual, there was no small talk with Devon. He cut straight to the heart of things.

"I don't know," April answered. "To be honest, we didn't talk about you."

"But it sure seemed that way, didn't it?"

"I guess so. I'm sorry." April twirled the combination of her lock and pulled the door open. "Devon, do you ever feel that you're . . . I don't know . . . sort of skating or something, and you can't stop? I mean, you glide right past things you want to stop and change, but . . ."

"Wow." Devon let out a low whistle. "Is that how you feel?"

She nodded. Without a bit of warning, tears began to sting her eyes.

"April," Devon whispered. He stepped closer, frowning.

She looked away. "I'm sorry. This is really embarrassing."

"Hey." Devon touched her arm, then her chin, cupping it with his fingers. "It's okay. Do you need to talk? Once in a while the principal can be cool. Maybe he'll give you the period off."

April shook her head. "I'm all right. I just—"

Devon's hands dropped to her shoulders. He stroked them with his thumbs. "Listen, I don't want to be a problem for you." He slipped his hands into his pockets. "Between you and your mother."

"Oh, no!" April shook her head. "It's not you. Or—maybe it *was* you, yesterday. But there's a lot more to it." She took a deep breath.

Surrounding them was the usual noise and clatter of the halls between periods. Locker doors slamming, people yelling, footsteps hurrying past. A few months before, April had hated Langley. Now it was almost a refuge for her. Mom had withdrawn again into another blue mood. It wasn't as bad as before, but it was there.

137

April had been trying to ignore it. She didn't want to think about it.

"Devon," she said, "maybe I need . . . to get away. Just for a day. What if we go to the coast Saturday?"

"The coast? Wait a second. I thought your mother—"

April shook her head. "I've done every single thing my mother wanted. I didn't want to leave Covington, or live in that apartment, or go to this school. But I've done it. Now I want to go to the coast with you Saturday. That can't be too much to ask, can it? I want to smell the ocean and feed the gulls and build a sand castle. Be . . . you know . . . be not serious."

Devon grinned. "You're picking *me* for this?"

Sniffing up a tear, April grinned back. "Hey, you know how to blow bubbles."

"Well, I'm not the one you'll have to convince." He gave her a skeptical look.

At home during dinner, Devon's words played through April's mind. He was right—the person she had to convince was sitting across the table from her at that moment. It would be anything but easy.

After the meal, she felt glad for once that it was her turn to help on the kitchen cleanup. That gave her and her mother some time alone, with Sean safely out of earshot in his room.

She picked up a clean glass to wipe dry, gathering all her courage.

"Things have been going great at school," she said as casually as she could.

Mom gave a little smile, not looking away from the saucepan she was scrubbing. "Your report card was very good last semester. I'm glad our move hasn't affected your grades."

April nodded. "But I mean, other things, too. Like, I have a lot of friends now at Langley. I was afraid at first that I would never find any."

"Of course you would, sweetheart."

"On Friday afternoon, a bunch of kids are going to see a play in Vickers Oaks. Can I go? Mason can take me."

"Oh, the boy in the S.D.L.? The one I met at the holiday bazaar? That sounds fine."

April took a deep breath. "And on Saturday, I want to go to the coast."

"With Mason?" Mom asked.

"With Devon." April started on a second glass.

"Devon." Mom squinted at the saucepan.

"Yes. Devon Riddley. You met him yesterday out-side—"

"I know who Devon is," Mom interrupted.

"Can I go?"

Mom set the pan on the drain board, looked up at April, then wiped her hands on a dish towel. "I wonder if you're deliberately trying to provoke an argument with me."

April frowned. "Provoke an argument? Mom, I just—"

"Let's sit down," her mother said.

They slid into chairs on opposite sides of the kitchen table.

"There are several different kinds of people in this world, April. There are people who are going some-where, and there are others who are not. I met the boy yesterday, and I can see what kind of person he is."

"What kind is he?" April asked angrily, steaming inside.

Mom sighed, pushing her hair behind her ears. "I don't want you going out with him. I didn't say anything yesterday because I thought you got my message. You know you defied my wishes just by riding home with someone I hadn't met. Frankly, I was too tired to take you on about the issue yesterday. I've given you my an-swer, and you'll just have to accept it."

For a moment April stared at her mother. She counted to ten, trying to calm herself down. In an article in one of the teen magazines about negotiating with parents, it said to ask polite questions, listen carefully to the answers, and bring up positive points in your favor. Be reasonable, act adult.

"Mom," she began, "I'd like to know how you made your decision about Devon."

Her mother shook her head. "I met him. I saw him."

"That's right. You *saw* him. You didn't talk with him, or learn anything about him."

"I can see," Mom retorted, "that he's not . . ." She paused. "April, listen. You have a place in this world. A place *that* boy will never reach."

April felt stunned. Only after several seconds did she find her voice. "Is it his hair, Mother? His car? The earring? Is that how you decided on Devon's whole personality?"

Mom's face grew stiff. "I want you to have friends, April. I'm delighted that you're getting along well at Langley. But there are dangers, and I'm not going to let you fall into them. I don't want you mixing up with the crowds at that school."

April huffed out a breath. "You mean the *wrong* crowds, don't you? If it's the S.D.L., if it looks to you like a Covington clone, it's okay, right? But if it's the least bit different—"

"Hold on, April," Mom cut in. "That's not fair. Your friend Yoko is different. Yet she's very nice. I accept that Langley isn't Covington. But your time here is going to be short. You may have to finish high school at Langley, but then you'll go to a good college somewhere else. You shouldn't get too involved here."

April's stomach turned. She felt more hurt—even sick—than she would have thought possible. How could her mother say such things?

Maybe this was what Dad had meant about Covington. Narrow minds, narrow thinking. Maybe her own mother had been choked by it, and she didn't even know.

Chapter 13

"I think I understand, Mother," April finally said, slowly and carefully. She looked straight at her mother across the kitchen table. "You want me to have *some* friends here, but not too many, and only the right ones. And I shouldn't get too close to them, anyway. Is that it?"

Mom just stared back.

"Let's see," April went on. "You want me to float through Langley like a ghost. Not get too attached. Or like a princess—too good for the lowlife, right?"

"April, I don't appreciate your sarcasm."

April exploded. "You're a snob!" She was shocked by the force of her own voice, which had risen to a shout. "Look, it wasn't my idea to leave Covington and live here. *I* didn't lose the house, okay?"

Lying beside her on the linoleum, Ranger whined. He hated family arguments. But April couldn't stop. Months of dammed-up rage and resentment flooded out. *"I'm* not the one who messed up on paying the bills and got us stuck here. This was all your idea. You can't sit there now and tell me how to run my life. You just can't!"

Eyes locked on her mother's, April saw that Mom was angry, too. But deeper than that, there was pain in Mom's eyes. A big, hurting lump rose in April's own throat. At any moment her welling tears would overflow. She hated feeling this way—furious and helpless. She could yell at her mother all she wanted, accomplishing nothing more than making Mom more and more angry at her, and more and more hurt. In the end, nothing would change.

Slowly, April stood up and walked out of the kitchen. In her room, she collapsed on the bed and buried her face in a pillow, trying to smother her sobs.

Please leave me alone, she pleaded silently, wishing she had locked the door. She couldn't face talking to her mother anymore. But Mom didn't even try to come in.

During the next couple of days April felt she and her mother were walking on eggshells. Neither of them mentioned the argument again. In fact, they hardly spoke at all.

Sean tried to take up the slack at dinnertime, talking about a girl's spectacular nosebleed at recess that day and the Siamese cat that Ranger had tried to chase during his walk the day before. More than once April caught a worried, bewildered look on her little brother's face, as if he wanted to fix things between his sister and mother, but had no idea how.

At school, when Devon asked April about the trip to the beach, she told him she couldn't go, even though she was beginning to think she *should* go, no matter what Mom said. What was the worst her mother could do? Yell at her? Ground her? It couldn't be much worse than how things were already going.

Never before had April defied her mother. At least, not about anything so important. And she really didn't want to start now.

Friday morning she called Toby.

"Well, hello, stranger!" Toby boomed. "Why are you calling so early? I've been planning to call you all week but I got busy with the photography club. How's it going?"

"Lousy," April confessed.

"Oh? I thought things were—"

"They were. Now they're not. Can I spend the weekend at your house?"

"Hey, sounds great. Well, great for me, anyway. But it sounds like you need a *real* vacation."

"Exactly. I've got some thinking to do."

"I'm not sure how good my house will be for that," Toby warned. "It's not what you'd call tranquil around here."

"Your parents?"

"Mmm-hmm." Toby sighed. "Cats and dogs. Maybe they'll cut it out if there's company here."

"Anything would be better than this," April assured her.

Right away, Mom okayed the weekend stay with Toby, as if she were relieved, too, to have a vacation from her daughter. April tried not to take it personally, but that afternoon she couldn't really concentrate on *Candida,* the George Bernard Shaw play she saw with Mason and the other S.D.L. people. Even their joking around at a pizza place afterwards didn't seem as funny as usual.

When Mason dropped her off at the Covington shopping mall, where she had arranged to meet Toby, April smiled. "I really appreciate the ride out here, Mason. And the invitation today. I had a great day."

"You sure? You haven't seemed exactly . . . up." Mason raised an eyebrow.

She shrugged. "Sorry."

"Hey, no apologies. Just . . . are you okay?" Mason asked.

"I'm fine. Ups and downs. Everybody has them, I guess."

"Okay. If you need anything, though . . ."

"Thanks. I'll be all right."

He gave her a honk and a wave as he drove away.

Walking into the mall, April felt better, even though her eyes had gone steamy. It seemed she could cry at the drop of a hat these days. This time it had been Mason's concern that set her off. But having friends again—real friends who cared—made all the difference. She realized that this particular set of tears were more or less happy ones.

"Hey, it's not that bad, is it?" a voice asked when she reached the entrance to the Palace department store. Toby held a thumb-sized brown teddy bear out to her. "This is for you. Found him at the card shop. Isn't he cute?"

April hugged the fuzzy toy to her chest. "Oh, Toby, he's wonderful." Then she hugged Toby, too. "So are you."

"Uh-oh. Looks like this is going to be what they call a 'tearful reunion.' "

April laughed through a sniffle. "Believe it or not, I'm very, very happy right now. Thanks for the bear. What's his name?"

After a long discussion, a short argument, and a lot of giggling, they decided on "Chuck."

"Short for Charlie," Toby said, pretending to swoon. "As in Sheen."

For an hour they wandered up and down both sides of the mall, faking British accents in the Mod Modes Boutique, making faces into store security cameras, and tossing pennies into the wishing-well fountain in the mall's center.

Finally they collapsed in the frozen-yogurt shop with brimming waffle cones.

"Boy," April murmured, taking a big slurp at her cone. "I feel better."

"It's the Peach Delight," said Toby. "Always does the trick."

"I was feeling better even before the Peach Delight. Being with you, back here again . . ."

"Does Covington still feel like home?"

April shrugged. "In a way. It definitely feels safe.

144

Sort of, I don't know, as if I don't have to worry about things here."

"What things do you have to worry about in Easton?"

April kept licking her frozen yogurt. She didn't want to answer Toby. If she did, it would kill her mood—the safe and calm feeling. It would disappear like a popped bubble. Again.

"Want to see a movie?" Toby asked. "That new mystery is playing here. The one with that awesome Australian hunk."

April shook her head.

"Oh, hey, if you didn't bring enough cash, I can pay." Toby studied her cone as if it were the most fascinating thing in the world. She was frowning a little, looking hesitant, maybe embarrassed.

At that moment April realized that Toby knew. She must know what had been worrying April for months: money, and what would happen if Mom ran out of it.

April longed to pour her heart out to her friend, to tell her everything. But Toby, whose wallet always held a couple of twenty-dollar bills, couldn't possibly understand.

"Would you rather just walk around some more?" Toby suggested. "The mall doesn't close till ten tonight."

"Sorry I'm such a dud." April sighed.

"April." Toby leaned forward and looked at her. "You're my friend."

For a long moment they just sat there, frozen yogurt slowly melting onto their napkins.

April nodded. "I know."

"Then why haven't you told me what's going on?" Toby questioned. "What the heck happened?"

"Nothing in particular." April shook her head. "Or maybe it was just the last straw. A guy I met."

"Oh! Devon? From New Year's Eve?" Toby asked excitedly.

As they finished their cones April explained how strongly she felt about Devon, how strongly her mother opposed him, and the horrible, painful argument they'd had.

"She *said* that?" Toby's eyes went wide. "She said you're too good for the kids at Langley?"

"Not in so many words," April admitted, "but that's what she meant. It's as if Mom won't one hundred percent accept that we don't live in Covington anymore. She wants to keep parts of us in Covington. Our hearts and minds or something. To keep things the way they were. She's really scared, I think. I guess she feels guilty, too."

"About losing the house and everything?" Toby nodded. "I know *I'd* feel guilty."

"But if I were her," April countered, "I'd feel even more guilty about saying snobby, dumb things about people I didn't know, like what she said about Devon. It's just his appearance she's going on, because he's not a preppie or a jock. She's decided he's a Hell's Angel or something."

"I think you need to talk to her."

"It's so hard, Toby."

"I know, but . . . it sounds like your mother's as miserable as you are."

April looked up.

"Know what I mean?" Toby asked. "Look, you said yourself she seems scared. I wouldn't want to be in her shoes, that's for sure. Trying to raise kids alone, plus feeling guilty about moving them to a bad neighborhood and everything. Sounds rotten."

"Whose side are you on?" April frowned. "Why are you defending her?"

"Hey, relax. I'm just saying that if she's as depressed as you are, you've got something in common, right? I mean, you're not at completely opposite ends."

April shrugged. "I hadn't thought of it that way."

"Let's walk some more, okay? Exercise. I can already feel the calories scouting out my thighs."

As they cruised the mall, Toby said, "Your mom's not being fair about your social life. You've got to talk to her."

"But we always end up fighting."

"Yeah. That's the hard part. Staying calm. I wish my parents knew how."

"Is their fighting that bad?"

"Oh, sometimes I think it's the end, you know. Divorce time. But it's always about such stupid stuff. Who left the milk out or who forgot to pay the gardener or whatever. Then they make up and everything's great. For at least half an hour." Toby laughed.

That was the most April had ever heard about Toby's family problems. Maybe, like her, Toby had always wanted to talk about them, but hadn't known if April would understand.

"Fighting is such a pain," Toby sighed. "Do me a favor, okay? Try not to do it too much with your mom. I think maybe it gets to be a habit. Look, how about if you even told your mother that? Something like, 'Mom, I'm tired of fighting. Let's try to talk.' "

April gave her a half-grin. "Would you come referee?"

"Not on your life!" Toby shook her head emphatically.

The next day was truly a vacation. They stayed in bed late, then Toby's father made waffles. As Toby had predicted, her parents were on their best behavior around April.

In the afternoon the girls played tennis at the community center, then went to Lauren's house for a barbecue.

April spent the whole day without one thought about her problems. She needed that. She even needed the fake but powerful Covington feeling that everything was okay and that there was no hunger or homelessness in the world. Even if there were, it seemed it would never reach Covington.

That night in the twin beds in Toby's room, the two of them lay awake laughing about Wilsey's brother Jake and how dumb he had acted around Lauren at the barbecue. He had suddenly gone nuts over her after her election to the Pep Squad.

Toby was doing a hilarious imitation of him when muffled shouts interrupted her.

"Oh, Lord," Toby whispered. "There they go."

April lay silent, listening to the voices coming from the master bedroom down the hall. She couldn't understand what Toby's parents were saying, but it was clear that they were angry with each other.

"Guess I should just get earplugs, huh?" Toby joked.

"Toby." April swallowed. "I . . . you never really told me much about this before. I mean, your parents. I hope that if you ever, you know, want to talk . . ."

"Thanks," said Toby quietly.

"I mean it."

"Sometimes I think," Toby began, sighing, "that if I had brothers and sisters, it would be easier. At least to have somebody to sympathize with. And maybe Mom wouldn't pick on me so often about my weight, either. She'd be too distracted by the other kids. Safety in numbers or something. So, it's good to know. About you . . . being around."

"It's good to know about you, too," April answered.

After a while the shouting died down. Toby's words came back into April's head: *Safety in numbers.* She did feel safe with Toby. Although Toby was one of her oldest, closest friends, it seemed she hadn't truly started to know her until that day. Before, Toby had been a fun pal, someone to hang around with. Once in a while she'd been a shoulder to cry on. April had never expected much more than that. Not from someone in Covington.

Not real understanding about living in a shabby apartment and feeling scared. But that was exactly what Toby had offered.

At home on Sunday, April resolved to take her friend's advice. All evening she looked for the right moment to talk to her mother. The longer she waited, the more nervous she got.

She was sitting on the floor in her room with Ranger's head in her lap, thinking about calling Toby for a shot of courage, when Mom walked in.

"Hi," Mom said.

"Hi."

"Did you have a good time at Toby's?"

April nodded. "I've missed her a lot."

"We missed you, too, this weekend." Mom sat in April's desk chair, swiveling it back and forth. She wore an old gray sweatsuit and a tired smile. Recently April had begun to notice the crow's-feet around her mother's eyes. She seemed to have more wrinkles than she had a few months ago. Maybe it was because she couldn't get her facials anymore, or buy the expensive cosmetics she used in Covington.

"You missed me?" April asked.

Mom rubbed the wooden edge of the chair back with her palm. "I did. And I didn't like the way we left things last week."

April shook her head. "Neither did I."

"Can we talk about it?"

"I was going to ask you the same thing," April confessed.

A brighter smile lit Mom's eyes. "Well, in that case, I want you to know . . . I didn't mean everything I said the other day. A lot of the things I said were . . . off the cuff. Sometimes I'm just not thinking straight these days, sweetheart. Can you understand that?"

April bit her lip. "Yes. Oh, Mom. I'm so glad."

"That I'm not thinking straight? Thanks." Mom grinned.

"No." April laughed. "That you didn't mean that stuff. I just couldn't believe you were the kind of person who thought that way."

"Then you don't really feel I'm a snob?"

April shrugged a shoulder. "It sure sounded that way."

"I am a snob in some ways," Mom admitted. "I want only the best for my children. That makes me quite snobby, because what's good enough for some just isn't good enough. But I don't want to be the kind of person who . . . chooses people like furniture. You were right about a couple of things, April. I made a snap judgment about your friend Devon, and I may have been wrong."

April felt shocked. "Really?"

"Well, you tell me. Was I?"

April hesitated. If she were to tell her mother everything she knew about Devon, Mom could decide she had been right, after all. The alternative was to tell Mom only the good parts—how serious Devon was, how he talked *with* her and not just at her like most boys did, how he really listened and cared. Other people had said he was nice, too. And then there was his award in math, not to mention that his mother wrote for the newspaper.

April could tell her mother only those things. But what if Mom found out about the rest of Devon later? About Kip Roemer and the court and juvenile detention?

"Well, you were right in a way," April finally said. "Devon is different from other boys I've been friends with." She listed all of his good points.

Mom listened, nodded, and once in a while smiled.

April took a breath. It was now or never. Devon's past might turn Mom completely against him. Or maybe Mom would be willing to give him a chance.

She decided to gamble. As she explained Devon's

background, her mother kept listening and nodding, but didn't smile nearly as often as she had before.

At the end, Mom rested an elbow on the chair back. "That's quite a story."

"I know. I was pretty surprised when I heard it, too," April said, "because Devon doesn't act anything like that anymore."

"Of course," said Mom.

April wasn't sure she liked the sound of that remark.

"Did he tell you all this?" her mother asked.

April nodded. "Yoko and BeeBee told me first, then he explained it all."

"At least he's honest."

"Definitely," April agreed.

"You're honest, too, sweetheart. I appreciate that. It's very important to me that we be open with each other."

April nodded. Her heart pounded with anticipation. What would Mom say? In the back of her head, there was yet another question. Could she and Mom be honest with each other about other things now? For instance, money? Their future? Dad?

"How were you planning to get to the coast?" Mom asked.

April couldn't believe her ears. She felt like whooping. But instead she pulled her mind away from the other problems she had been thinking about and concentrated on the one at hand.

"Devon has a car. You probably saw it that day. It—"

"It looks horrible."

"It runs fine. More or less."

"I want you two to take the bus."

April's eyes widened. "To the coast? You mean, we can go? This Saturday?"

"The city runs a shuttle from Washington Street to the beach village every hour on weekends. I've read about it in the paper. They're trying to develop boardwalk businesses. It's cheaper than the gas would be, anyway."

"We can go?" April repeated, hardly able to contain herself.

Mom closed her eyes and nodded. "You can go."

April leaped to her feet and threw her arms around her mother.

Mom hugged back, then held April away to look at her. "I'm trusting your judgment. Make sure you remember that."

"This is perfect." April sighed, digging her fingers into the sand.

Devon lay beside her in the bright sunlight, their heads propped up on a driftwood log so that they could gaze out at the ocean.

A few feet away, three toddlers kicked at a beach ball. The warm air was filled with their laughter, a jazzy song from someone's radio, and the gentle lapping of the waves on the shore.

"You picked a great day for this," Devon said. "February can be really rotten out here."

"The weather wouldn't dare give me a hard time," April said. "Not today."

"This was really important to you, wasn't it? To get your mom to let you go out with me?"

April rolled over on her stomach. She let a handful of sand sift through her fingers. "Yes."

"Me, too. Thanks. I mean, for convincing her." He grinned. "I thought I was going to have to send her reference letters or something."

April grinned back. "Almost."

"Are you glad you went to the trouble?" He shaded his eyes from the sun, squinting at her.

"What do you think?" April grabbed another handful of sand and deposited it very gently on Devon's chest.

"Hey!" he yelped, reaching for her arm.

Giggling, April jumped up and ran as fast as she could down the beach.

Within seconds Devon was there, too. Salvos of damp sand pelted her shoulders and hips.

"Hah! Got you!" Devon crowed.

April reached down for fresh ammunition. "You're sunk, Riddley!"

They chased each other up and down the beach, laughing so hard that most of their shots missed. People stared, and at one point a rogue wave caught them and drenched them both to their thighs, but April didn't care.

"That water's *freezing,*" Devon complained. "I think I've got fish in my shoes."

"Here, lean on my shoulder and take them off," April suggested.

Devon complied, and in a moment they were walking barefoot at the surf's edge, holding hands.

The ocean's icy bite on April's skin began to thaw. The sun on her face, the warm sand between her toes, and the delicious thrill of Devon's fingers twined with hers made her feel it was the middle of a long summer.

She squeezed his hand tighter and looked at him. "This doesn't seem real."

"It does to me," Devon answered. "Very real." After a moment he asked, "Do you remember New Year's Eve?"

April nodded. "Hard to forget. The only bubble-blowing lesson I've ever had."

Devon made a face. "Gave *me* an ulcer."

"Blowing bubbles?"

"I was petrified," he said.

"Of what?"

"Of you. Of sounding stupid. Of turning you off."

"Really?" April cocked her head.

"Yeah, really."

April's heart took a happy little leap. But then she said, "Don't tell me you're shy, Riddley. I've heard stories about you. Sounds like there aren't too many girls at Langley who haven't noticed you."

"Thanks for the compliment. What stories?"

"Oh, you're just fishing for *more* compliments, aren't you? Do you really want to hear all the juicy gossip?"

"If it's about me, sure I do. Wait, let me guess. The Ice Prince stuff?"

"You've heard about that?" April blushed. She got the feeling that she was more embarrassed by Devon's nickname than he was.

But he blushed, too. "There's a reason for it, you know. I don't . . . string girls along, like they say."

"What do you do, then?"

He kicked at a stick of driftwood, then looked at her. "I've just been waiting."

April felt a warm tingling in her belly. She remembered Devon's words on New Year's Eve. *I've been waiting for you.*

"You think I'm snowing you again," he said.

"Are you?"

"Want the facts?" He picked up the driftwood and turned it over and over in his hands. "Okay. Here they are. Things happen too fast sometimes. And lots of people don't care what's happening, as long as it's happening, you know? There are kids—kids I know—who have fried out on crack, or smashed up in cars, or gone to bed with anyone and everyone who turned up. That's not what *I* want."

He threw the stick so hard it whistled through the air. It landed far away on the waves, breaking the gray surface with a splash.

"My parents," Devon went on, "are . . . what's the word? Eccentric? Leftover hippies. They can't help it." He grinned. "But they care a lot, too. As bad as it's ever gotten, the worst it *ever* got for me, they were there. I knew I had them with me. So that's what I want for the rest of my life, too. I want things to be real. Not

154

just some girl who happens to look good at the time. Do you know what I mean?''

April's heart was thudding now. His eyes were fixed on hers, dark yet full of light.

"So there it is. The excuse for my rep."

"It's quite a rep." April half-smiled, trembling, trying not to let him see it. "Unique, I guess."

"I guess." Devon put his hands in his pockets.

They walked for what seemed like miles. April felt as if she were in a dream. Yet she knew she couldn't be mistaken about what Devon had tried to tell her. She just didn't know what to say to him about it. But then, she didn't really have to say anything, did she? He hadn't asked her for an answer.

As they strolled down the beach they talked about whales and lighthouses. April realized there was no pressure. Somehow, Devon had made it clear he wasn't expecting anything. She knew in her heart exactly what he meant. It went along with the kind of person he was—intense, serious, honest—not the type to hold anything back.

He just wanted her to know.

Chapter 14

Climbing the stairs to the apartment Saturday afternoon, April felt so light she thought she could float up instead. Her arms and legs were dandelion fluff, and her head was entirely cotton candy.

Devon had walked with her down Wilcox Avenue after they got off the bus from the coast, and for those few minutes it had seemed like the loveliest street in the world. Even the Easton Arms looked gracious.

He had kissed her at the door of the building, just a light, quick touch, but a kiss anyway. Their first.

April sprinted up the last flight of stairs to the fourth floor, realizing that she was beyond happy. Delirious was more like it. That's what Yoko would say, anyway. *Cov, you've gone ditzy over the dude. You're in his back pocket. Call 911.*

Mom would take one look at her flushed nose and cheeks and say she had gotten too much sun.

April, though, knew the sun and even Devon weren't entirely responsible for making her feel so good. Maybe she *was* ditzy over him, and maybe she hadn't worn enough sunscreen. But more important, for the first time in months, she felt she had her life together. The future actually looked bright.

Making the trip to the beach with Devon had meant not only that she'd won some independence from her mother, but also that things might be better now between her and Mom. Maybe they were learning how to talk with each other and iron out their differences. Then there were all the other good things that had happened recently: rebuilding her friendship with Toby, finding great friends in Yoko and Mason, even achieving some goals in the S.D.L. Top it off with a dreamy day on the beach with an incredible guy, and she was over the edge.

Humming, she took her keys out of her pocket and headed down the hall. She was halfway to the apartment when she heard Ranger barking and noticed the building manager standing outside the door.

"Oh, hi, Mrs. Kriss. How are you?"

"I'm fine. I need to speak with your mother. I've been knocking all day and no one answers. Just that dog." The woman's thin, deeply wrinkled face looked pinched. Her lips pursed tight and her painted-on eyebrows frowned.

"We've all been out today." April glanced at her watch. "Mom and Sean should be back in about an hour, though. They went shopping for—"

Mrs. Kriss interrupted with a grunt. "Your mother shouldn't be shopping for anything." Another grunt. Her lips pursed even tighter.

"What?" April frowned. "Why not?"

From the pocket of her brown cardigan the woman pulled a stack of envelopes. "This is why. Your mother owes me three months' worth of electricity."

"Three months?" April echoed.

Mrs. Kriss pushed at the back of her heavily teased black hair with a finger. "Sorry, dear. I can't go on this way. The rental agreement says that I pay gas and water, and renters pay electric through me. I did what I could. I've carried your mother's electric bills because I believe in giving people a little extra chance, you know? Besides, she's been giving me the rent. But she promised she'd give me the payments this week, and she didn't."

"Maybe . . . maybe she'll give them to you today," April stammered.

"I can't go on 'maybe's.' " The woman tapped the bills on her palm. "I can't front it anymore, understand? I'll have to let the utility shut you off if I don't get what I'm due. You tell your mother that, all right?"

April felt breathless, as if a brick had hit her in the chest. "You'll shut off our lights?"

"*I* won't, but the power company will. Don't look at *me,* dear. I'm sorry. I did what I could. You just tell your mother." Mrs. Kriss handed April the envelopes and hurried away.

Slowly, April unlocked the apartment door. Ranger greeted her with a whine and a tail wag. She ignored him, locking the door behind her. Then she found her way to the sofa and sat down.

157

Some things were possible, she thought, and others were not. For most of her life she had believed that certain things could never happen. She hadn't known how shaky the ground beneath her really was—how very, very easily it could simply crumble away and leave her falling, tumbling through thin air. She and her mother and Sean had been falling all year, and April hadn't been able to do anything to stop it.

Ranger brought her a tennis ball.

"Thanks," she whispered, petting him. She tossed the ball across the room for him.

He brought it back and rested his chin on her knee.

In spite of the cold knot in her stomach, she smiled. "Some things never change, do they, boy?"

He wagged his tail and followed April to her room. She opened the top dresser drawer. Under the pile of socks she found the envelope.

"You'll have to stay here," she told Ranger as she unlocked the apartment door. "Don't worry. I'll be right back. After I launch a parachute."

"Where did you get the money?"

That was the first question Mom asked that evening when April told her she had paid Mrs. Kriss.

"I had it saved up," April said, careful not to lie. She *had* been saving the money from Lacey for an emergency just like this one.

"Why didn't you consult me?"

"You weren't here."

"April, don't double-talk me. You know what I'm saying. How could you just go off and—"

"*Some*body had to do it, Mom."

A strange sound came from her mother's mouth—half hiss, half groan—as if she had started to say something, then pulled it back.

April knew her mother was more than angry. Furious. She could tell by the iron-stiff set of her shoulders.

158

They sat in the living room alone. Sean was across the hall playing video games with a neighbor boy.

Finally, Mom sighed. "I know you were doing what you thought best, April. And I thank you for that. It was very responsible of you. But you are not responsible for this family. *I* am."

Then why don't you act like it? April wanted to scream, but didn't. She remembered Toby's advice. Toby was right. There was no reason to argue with Mom, at least not about this. They were on the same side.

"Mom, you're not the only person responsible for us."

"You are fifteen years old, April," Mom began. "It's not your place to deal with the building manager or—"

"I don't mean *me*, Mom," April said quietly.

Her mother seemed to feel the force behind April's words. She took a breath and leaned back in her chair.

"Sean and I have two parents, not just one," April pointed out. "You can't do this all by yourself right now. You shouldn't have to, either."

Mom sat in silence. Her mouth was a brittle line.

"I know Dad has expenses," April began, "but—"

"The baby was just born," her mother whispered.

"I know that. I'm not saying Dad's rich. But he has enough. He's got to start sending you what he's supposed to."

Mom let out a short, joyless laugh. Then she began studying the place mat, smoothing the ruffled edges with her fingers. "Marriage," she said, pausing. "It's such a funny thing."

April bit her lip. She hated seeing the pained, deflated look on her mother's face.

"When your father and I divorced," Mom said, "we hadn't stopped loving each other. Did you know that?" She shook her head. "We just—we didn't want the same things anymore, I guess. I don't know how that can pull two people apart, but it can."

"I love you both, Mom," April told her. "It doesn't matter to me anymore that you and Dad got a divorce. I just want for things to work out."

Her mother reached out and cradled April's hand in hers. "I know, sweetheart. I know you do. I just think I . . . I need to explain this to you. Last week I admitted I was wrong about something. Now I'm going to admit another mistake: I had no idea how upset you were."

"About—" April hesitated, then found her courage again. She had to get all this out in the open. "About our money problems?"

Mom nodded. "I know you've tried to tell me in a number of different ways." Her eyes brimmed with tears.

April squeezed her hand and whispered, "Please don't cry."

Mom forced a smile. "I've been thinking about this whole situation for quite some time, April. It's not just today. *You're* not making me cry. Actually, I . . ." She sniffled and blew her nose with a paper napkin. "I feel . . . freed."

In a vague way, April thought she knew what her mother was trying to say. She waited.

"I'm only sorry," Mom went on, "that *you* paid the price." She looked straight at her daughter. "I'm very, very sorry, April. I didn't know it would go this way. I really didn't. People do things—*I* did—believing they are absolutely right. There was no doubt in my mind. I wanted to be independent. I wanted to get along splendidly without your father. To prove—to him *and* to myself—that I didn't need him in any way. The support payments were my last ties to him. If only I could break them . . ."

"Oh, Mom. Getting money from Dad is nothing to be ashamed of. We're *his* kids, too. He owes it to us."

Mom nodded. "I know he does. And he knows he does. But he's still angry with me, and here was one way he could—'' Suddenly she stopped. "I'm sorry. I don't mean to criticize your father."

A little laugh escaped April. "Criticize him? If I were you I'd be ready to *clobber* him."

Mom shook her head. "I'm not. I've played the game as hard as he has. Don't be angry with your father, sweetheart. Or with me. Please?" She took April's hands in both of hers. "I am making a promise to you. Things are going to change. Your father and I are going to have a talk."

"You are?"

"A long talk." Mom sighed. "I'm not exactly looking forward to it, but it needs to be done."

April nodded. She felt tired, but deeply, deeply relieved. "Yes, Mom. It really does."

"Hey, remember that great soap fight we had in *your* kitchen Christmas Eve?" Yoko aimed a handful of suds at April.

Meemaw's wide, old-fashioned sink offered perfect ammunition.

Shielding herself with a dish towel, April pleaded, "No, not today! This is my embroidered Mexican blouse."

"You and your clothes," Yoko snorted.

"You and *your* clothes," April snorted back, poking at Yoko's latest thrift-shop find, a pair of red velveteen suspenders.

It had been a great day. Yoko had taken April on a tour of her favorite secondhand stores, then brought her home for lunch with Meemaw. Once again, April was amazed by her friend—how well she fit into two very different worlds. Tough enough to handle the gritty Easton streets, Yoko could then come home and slip into the role of loving granddaughter, speaking Japanese and respecting her grandmother's old-country customs.

Being with Yoko all day had helped keep April's mind

161

off other things. Mom and Dad were supposed to be having their big talk today. That morning April had ridden the bus with Sean to his friend Damon's house. Then she rode it on to Yoko's so that Mom could have some privacy on the phone.

Mentally, she crossed her fingers.

"You know, Cov, you should be nice to me," Yoko claimed, rinsing a platter. "You owe me."

"Oh, I do? For what?"

"Who took you to the party where you met Mr. Wonderful?"

April rolled her eyes.

"You're blushing. Hah, hah. But it's okay. At least you're not totally wigged out over him. I mean, you've got a speck or two of gray matter left in your brain. That's good. I hate it when people totally lose it."

"Glad you approve," April grunted.

"Yeah, well, somebody's gotta keep an eye on you. For a while there, I was wondering. You weren't exactly the picture of joy at Langley. I didn't want you to fall into the paws of the first guy who showed you some affection."

"Hey, I wasn't *that* pathetic," April protested. "But . . . you're right about one thing. I do owe you."

"Yeah?"

"Yeah." April nodded. "You were my first friend at Langley. I didn't know it at the time, but . . ."

"Well, now we're making up for lost time, right?"

April nodded again. "Right."

While finishing the dishes, they talked about BeeBee's new boyfriend, Greg, and Yoko's most recent set of simultaneous crushes on three different boys in her biology class. April realized that this was probably the same kind of thing she would have been doing on a Saturday if she still lived in Covington, except she would have been with Toby or Lauren instead of Yoko. Maybe it wouldn't have been so bad to have spent all her Saturdays in Covington. But she just couldn't imagine that now. She couldn't imagine not having met Yoko or Mason or Devon. Or Mazie or Meemaw or Mr. Wortham. Or even, April thought ruefully, Mrs. Kriss.

They were all part of her life now—important parts.

Maybe, in that way, Dad was right. Maybe moving out of Covington was the best thing that could have happened to her and to Mom and to Sean.

One thing April knew for sure: she wouldn't trade her new friends, or the new person she herself had become, for a whole lifetime anywhere else.

April yawned. The school library was overheated. Late February weather had gone wacky, warming up to spring-like temperatures, but Langley custodians hadn't caught on. They kept the furnace blazing.

It made April sleepy. She wandered up and down the stacks, looking for the books by Jane Austen, hoping to find a good reading selection for the next tournament.

A librarian opened one of the windows nearby.

"Thanks," April whispered, fanning herself with her notebook.

Ms. Bertram nodded. "They're trying to roast us."

April decided that would make an original comedy skit for a speech tournament: school custodians attempting murder of students and staff through the thermostat.

She found the Jane Austen shelf. *Northanger Abbey, Pride and Prejudice, Sense and Sensibility.* April pulled the books into her arms. Mr. Wortham had said that Austen presented a big challenge to read well. But she felt ready for a challenge. She also wanted to be extra well-prepared for this tournament. Dad had said he might be in town then, and wanted to attend. With him in the audience, she knew she'd better do her absolute best, or else he'd spend all of spring break coaching her during their next visit.

She could hardly wait for the trip. She'd be meeting her little sister for the first time. Lacey sent new pictures of the baby almost every week. Everyone agreed that blond, rosy-cheeked Noelle looked just like April.

But while talking to Dad on the phone last weekend, she had felt, for only the second time in her life, awkward with him. She knew he had recently had the big discussion with Mom. She wondered if Mom had told him about April's involvement.

Part of her wanted to talk to Dad about the whole thing, to make sure he and Mom cooperated now, instead of playing out the divorce battle so many years later. But she stopped herself. Mom was right about something—taking care of the family was not April's job. It was her mother's and father's. She shouldn't have to get involved or worried or upset anymore. Maybe things wouldn't change right away, but April believed that they would soon.

Mom had already started keeping her promise. Not only had she talked with Dad, but she was also attending a class on personal financial planning offered at her office.

April carried the books to the table. There was a lot of work to do. Besides the S.D.L. tournament, she had midterm exams coming up in two weeks. In between there was palling around with Yoko and her friends, long phone conversations with Toby, and going out with Devon.

For a moment she let herself daydream about him. He was supposed to meet her in the library in half an hour.

She sighed. There just wasn't enough time for everything these days. Not that she meant to complain. It was quite an improvement over her early weeks at Langley, when she'd had far too much time on her hands.

"Why the frown?" Somebody dropped a load of books on the table.

April smiled up at Mason. "Just thinking. How's your debate research going?"

"Don't ask. That's why I'm here again. Keep hitting brick walls."

"What was your topic? AIDS?"

"That's part of it. I'm supposed to argue in favor of clean needles for drug addicts. A needle-exchange program run by government agencies. Addicts bring in dirty needles, get clean ones. It's supposed to help prevent AIDS."

April cocked her head sideways, thinking. "You've been through the Readers' Guide and all that stuff, I'm sure. You know, for a health class project last year I used this special medical index. The librarian showed it to me. Why don't you ask Bertram if they've got one here?"

Mason got up and bowed. "A thousand thanks, mademoiselle. I was about to throw in the towel." He paused, frowning. "By the way, where's your sidekick today?"

"Yoko?"

"No, the other one. The guy with the earring."

April rolled her eyes. "Mason, you know his name."

"Yeah, well . . ."

"Wait," April said. "Don't tell me you're going to start on me now. I just got Yoko over her phobia of Devon."

He shrugged. "I've been wondering . . . How serious are things between you two?"

April sighed. "I've always wondered what it would be like to have a big brother. Now I know."

Mason leaned over her, his fists pressing on the table. "A big brother." His voice went low. "Is that all you want me to be?"

April felt stunned. Mason's blue eyes focused on

165

her, demanding an answer. She couldn't give him one. For months she had suspected he might feel something more for her than friendship, but had always passed off her suspicions. Now, it seemed, she had been right.

The question remained: what *did* she want Mason to be?

"Mason, I . . ."

Out of the corner of her eye, April saw someone approaching. Devon stood at the other end of the table. He came no further.

His face was stony and unmoving—the statue. He took one look at Mason and April—how close they were, what a tender moment he seemed to have walked in on—and walked away.

"Hey!" Mason's voice boomed across the library.

Ms. Bertram frowned at him from her desk. "Quiet!" she hissed.

Devon turned around.

"Hey, pardner," Mason said quietly. "Ride on back over here." He sounded like a hero in the last scene of a Western movie, when he turns over the girl to the cowboy she really loves.

Devon walked back, but for a moment he and Mason just stood there, sizing each other up.

April swallowed hard. Of all the problems she'd faced this year, here was one she never expected.

Two guys. Two great guys.

Would she have to choose between them? Anyway, what about Mason and Sara?

One thing was for sure: *this* was the kind of problem she preferred. It was the kind that people her age were supposed to have—not electric bills and grocery money and paying the rent.

Just a few weeks ago she had felt as if she were falling out of control, plunging through thin air. Now it was different.

166

What to do when you're falling, April thought. She had learned that year. Open your eyes. Think. Send up your parachute.

Nowadays it felt more like skydiving—right into what just might be the best year of her life.

KATHRYN MAKRIS is the author of seventeen young adult and middle grades novels, including the *Almost Sisters* and upcoming *The Ecokids* series from Avon Books. Her first book was published when she was twenty-four years old.

As a reporter, Kathryn has covered hurricanes, capital murder trials, and Lego contests. She has hosted a radio talk show and has interviewed national personalities including the Rev. Jesse Jackson, Sissy Spacek, the real "Colonel" Sanders, and Benji the dog.

Raised in Texas in a family that spoke Greek and Spanish along with English, Kathryn now thrives on California's mix of cultures. She also enjoys flamenco dance, dogs, and almost anything outdoors.

Avon Flare Presents
THE WHITNEY COUSINS
by Award-Winning Author
JEAN THESMAN

*Three teenage girls dealing with
the complexity of growing up—*

HEATHER   75869-5/$2.95 US/$3.50 Can

For Heather, adjusting to a new stepfamily and new town is tough, especially at fifteen. But when her new stepsister's honesty is questioned, threatening her chances for a scholarship, Heather pulls for her, learning what it means to be a family.

AMELIA   75874-1/$2.95 US/$3.50 Can

When Warren, a handsome senior, takes Amelia out and tries to force her to go too far, Amelia is afraid to tell anyone because they might think she was "asking for it."

ERIN   75875-X/$2.95 US/$3.50 Can

Erin Whitney's parents were killed by a drunk driver when she was ten, and she's been shuffled from relative to relative ever since. But the Whitneys are a tough bunch and can see through to Erin's pain—making her feel, at last, that she has a real home.

TRIPLE TROUBLE   76464-4/$3.50 US/$4.25 Can

Amelia and Erin are staying with Heather for a summer of fun, adventure...and romance!